# Krigere & Voktere

# Book One:
# **The Relic**

TOLV WALSTAD

The Relic: Krigere & Voktere Book 1 © 2021 by Tolv Walstad

Copyright © 2021 by Tolv Walstad

Copyright © 2021 by Kriger and Vokter, LLC

All rights reserved.

ISBN: 978-1-958071-00-7

Published in the United States by Kriger and Vokter, LLC

Visit the Kriger and Vokter website to learn more

EX LIBRIS

𝕯elany

For my children, to always remember how important learning and reading are in life. And for my father, who was my all-time best cheerleader. I miss you, Dad.

Find out what's *on the horizon* and
*more about the author* on the author's website

# Prologue

Gorm gazed upon the mountain ranges and beautiful valley surrounding the castle as the peaks and fields gave way to the crystalline silence of the snowfall. He kept his black hair tied up in a knot with animal skin to keep the hair out of his face.

He embraced the cold wind; it made him feel alive. His green eyes focused on the distance, waiting as the nightfall began. He was eager to be gone from these castle walls—enough with hiding.

Over twenty years ago, he had escaped death from his people, all because of his unique gifts, among other things. During those years they'd recruited others like them to embrace their potential and had used the castle as their base of operations. Now they were ready to enact vengeance; only he knew that it was not time.

A guard stepped upon the wall beside him. "Thegn Gorm. Drott Agnar has asked to speak with you."

"I'll be along shortly." Gorm waved his hand to the guard to dismiss him.

The guard saluted and walked away.

Gorm knew what he wanted. It just depended on the messenger. Even the thought of it made his hands ball into fists. He couldn't start the war until he received word. The anticipation was getting to him, and he could feel the heat rising from his body. Each night he waited on the wall for the messenger to arrive.

Once again the time passed while he waited. It was going to be another one of those nights without news.

Gorm turned and started inside, then saw a glimmer in the distant horizon.

It was a raven, the long-awaited messenger. Months had passed since their last communication, and it had made him restless. A few guards had fallen to his anger during training; it was starting to manifest outwardly.

It felt like ages before the raven arrived. A light glow surrounded its body as it glided to the wall, a tightly rolled scroll in its claws.

Gorm's hand glided across the raven's spiritual back as it faded away, dropping the scroll upon the wall. He lifted the scroll and unrolled it.

> "No signs or indications that he has the relic. I have found nothing that looks like or resembles the relic. Even the markings we used failed. Please be informed that the festivities are about to begin, and any attempts beyond this point will take a long time before I can report again."

Once again, nothing. Agnar wasn't going to be happy with him. He slid the scroll restlessly into his pouch and turned toward the stairs. Agnar wasn't going to like the news.

Gorm walked the castle corridors, his eyes adjusting to the torchlight as it flickered against the wall, casting little shadows as it danced. The solid woodwork was beautiful. The walls were engraved with beasts of the fields and legend. Guards stood apart from each other, and some of them called their Fylgjur as he approached.

The Fylgjur had a special glow surrounding them, and their eyes were upon Gorm as he walked past them. Each of them stood beside their masters.

He knew he could call upon his Fylgja, but he didn't see the point. It made him smile to see the guards each salute him as he walked past. Intimidating them now would only irritate Agnar further. Gorm suspected that his conversation with Agnar would be the same as last time: no news, and they would have to wait before he could bring his betrayers to justice.

The guards opened the throne room doors to allow him entrance. Near the back of the room was the throne itself, flanked by two troll statues. Large wooden pillars stood in the shape of a U, moving from the door outward, opening up the room. On the right of the throne was a rock garden with a small pond. There a large man stood near its waters, and Gorm watched as a water nymph turned into mist at a wave of the man's hand.

"Welcome, Thegn Gorm." His deep voice sounded across the stones as he turned to greet him.

Gorm bent to one knee. "Drott Agnar." He bowed his head in respect.

"Come now. There is no time for pleasantries. I have a plan for us to attend to, but first, any news from your messenger?"

Gorm stood, and Agnar crossed to the throne. Gorm was not very eager to give the news. Agnar was larger than Gorm and stood taller. He had a human skull upon his left shoulder and armor made of scales down his right arm, and his white hair made him appear older than he was. His body was covered with armor and clothing made up of different scales, skins, and furs. His chest was exposed between them. Even being in the presence of Agnar made Gorm feel uneasy.

The silence passed between them for a moment until Agnar's light brown eyes met his own. "They have found nothing new, and with the festivities starting, our search will nearly come to a halt for some time," Gorm said.

"It isn't a shock that your spion hasn't found...

anything." Agnar let the word drag out as he sat down upon his throne.

Gorm was taken aback. He had been expecting Agnar to be angry with him. What angles had they not tried? They had spent years searching for the relic. His spion had done everything to find the relic. "Drott Agnar, you do not sound surprised."

Agnar gave a quick laugh and looked Gorm in the eyes. "I am not. The news doesn't surprise me, since I was finally able to break the prisoner. After all these interrogations, it became clear that it's been right there this entire time."

"The entire time? We searched all of his belongings. We tried sampling the branches around his arm; we even tried removing them. There is nothing that shows that the young man has the relic." Frustration was evident in Gorm's voice.

"This brings us to the business at hand. The young man needs to unlock his potential. Without it, we'll never get the relic."

"Are you saying that the boy is one of us?"

"That is what I am saying. His potential is just locked away." Agnar rose. "Gorm, inform your messenger that we are moving our plans up. Your time in the field has arrived. I need you to take a small regiment and show this young man his potential."

"Finally. How do we go about doing this, my Drott?" Gorm let the excitement escape his voice.

Agnar then detailed the plan to Gorm.

Gorm returned to the wall. The night was upon them, and the moon shone brightly against the snow-dusted valley. He pulled a small parchment from his pouch and inscribed the plan to his spion. Then he willed his Fylgja to appear. The spirit raven gazed into his eyes and knew what it had to do. Gorm rolled the scroll and watched the raven clutch it in its claws and fly into the distance.

His time had come—the waiting was over. Now was his chance to pass judgment upon those who had exiled him. He smiled as he embraced the cold wind. Winter was upon them.

# Chapter 1: Journey to the Warrior's Gate

The night gave way to starlight. From the valley it shone, down the hills to where it reflected across the lake. The water danced with the hue of firelight cast from the braziers throughout the village of Kjarra.

Men and women formed in groups around each brazier. The braziers created a path throughout the village, beginning at the lakeside and ending at the village gate.

The whole village was in attendance for the celebration of the Warrior's Gate. At their coming of age, each young adult passed through the Warrior's Gate to become a Kriger.

The day had begun with a series of trials to test each individual. The group of young adults by the lake awaited individual judgment from the elders and seers, and they would journey to each brazier to accept their fate. The question in all their minds was whether they had passed the trials in the true nature, along with characteristics of the Krigere. Only the journey would tell.

A boy nervously stepped side to side. "Anyone else nervous?" he asked. His long, light-brown hair was tied in a topknot. He ran his hands along the closely shaved sides of his head. He wore brown leather armor that covered his torso down to his legs. He had padded leather leggings and padded shoulders.

"No way, Erik. Those nervous butterflies in my stomach are just my eagerness getting the best of me. Can't wait to hear what they say," a blond girl said. She was slightly smaller than Erik by a few inches; she wore her hair down to her shoulders and tucked behind her ears. She wore black leather garb that covered her whole body from the neck down to her knees. She had thicker pads at her shoulders, with leather buckles to tighten them in place. Leather straps wrapped her arms for a more protective layer above the skin.

"It's deceiving to see you so calm about it all, Revna," he replied.

Another young man politely stepped through the crowd. "I'll never understand how you're nervous now, but during the trials, you kept your cool."

Revna smiled with her green eyes and gave the boy a slight shove on his shoulder. "Nice of you to join us, Tyr."

Tyr stood an inch taller than Erik, and his wavy brown hair shifted ever so slightly with the wind as he moved in to stand beside his friends. He wore leather armor as well, brown coverings over his chest and legs. His right arm was covered with a single shoulder pad with a leather buckle. Along his left bicep and moving up to his shoulder, branches were grafted into his skin.

They protruded in a tight-knit pattern; small holes allowed the skin underneath to be seen through the branches, which ran from shoulder to elbow. When he made eye contact with Revna, he knew that the butterflies in his stomach were from more than just awaiting judgment.

"Calm? You thought I was calm through all those trials? After meeting with the Seidr, I think I was in shock through the rest of it. Couldn't stop thinking about what they said," Erik replied.

Tyr thought of what they had said to him too, and it had been hard to concentrate after. "I know. Not sure why they put that as the first trial."

"Obvious, isn't it? Head games." Revna tapped her skull. "They start our day off by getting inside our heads and then put us to the difficult tasks."

"Guess they didn't say anything that could get to you, Revna," Erik said.

"Most of it is cryptic nonsense," she replied. "Though it's getting kind of boring out here, and we have some time to waste before it's our turn. Want to know what they told me?"

Tyr jumped in. "They said it was meant for us and sharing it would dilute its power."

"Guess we know what they said to you. 'Honorable. Law-abiding.'" Erik said the last words in a deep voice.

Tyr shook his head. "No, they said one friend had emotional issues."

"Not funny," Erik responded, then lunged forward to shove him. Tyr moved his left arm in front to soften the blow and rocked back on his heels.

"Sune, journey forth," the announcer called.

One boy stepped away from the crowd and started toward the first brazier.

"Anyone ever mentioned the Warrior's Gate to either of you?" Tyr asked.

"No, my parents never really were allowed to speak about it. Not knowing is part of the journey or something like that. Though that didn't stop me from asking about it over and over again. Still got nothing besides a good scolding." Erik waved his hand, scolding the air.

"My mor never said much to me either. It was the same way whenever I asked anything about my dad. It was all just kept secret," Revna said, her voice low and soft. "After a while, I just realized that there had to be a special reason she hadn't wanted to talk about it. Though I wish she were here to see me pass through the Warrior's Gate."

"Estrid, journey forth," the announcer called.

A girl stepped forward and started past the announcer to the first brazier. Up toward the second brazier, they could see the first boy arriving for the second part of the journey.

"We're here to see you pass through the Gate. You aren't alone." Tyr laid his hand on her shoulder.

"Appreciated," she replied and touched his hand with hers, then continued to stare toward the brazier.

"Even as kids, we tried to sneak toward the braziers and see what happened. To be fair, I think you got closer than anyone else, Tyr," Erik said.

"When Liv found out, she was angry for months. But after all these years and all the trouble we went through just to see the Warrior's Gate, we're finally here," Tyr responded.

"Revna, journey forth," the announcer called.

"Finally. I thought I was going to start floating off the ground with the number of butterflies in my stomach. Wish me luck." She turned and smiled at them and held up her hands with her fingers crossed.

They wished her good luck as she turned and walked toward the first brazier.

Tyr watched Revna arrive at the first brazier. Family members were gathered at each of the braziers, waiting for their son or daughter to journey forth. Then followed and supported them at the following braziers. But there was no one waiting for Tyr. He knew how Revna felt, making this journey alone. His whole life, he had been alone, an orphan with no past.

"Honestly can't take your eyes off of her, can you?" Erik waved his hand in front of Tyr's face.

Tyr blushed and turned his head. "Just thinking, that's all."

"She is gorgeous, strongheaded, and knows what she wants. No one knows where our lives will take us after these celebrations. My parents want me to settle down and continue with the tradition. Not sure what traditions we are trying to follow. From the stories we were told, we have had over fifteen years of peace in our lands, with the exception of a few raids and other mishaps along the way. Doesn't feel like much of a life to me."

Tyr didn't speak for a while. His mind raced through the moments in his past. The frustrations of growing up alone. Not knowing anything about his history—no mor—mother—and no far—father. The branches on his arm were a mystery to him, as was the small bag he had carried with him from childhood. None of it told the story. His voice came out stern then, determination in his voice. "There are a handful of things I plan on doing before I settle down. The main one is to figure out my past."

"Sorry, didn't mean to drag that up again. We can always continue where we left off and keep digging to figure out answers to the questions you have. Always happy to help." Erik tapped Tyr on the shoulder to reassure him.

Erik had been a good friend over the years. He and Tyr had gone through all of his belongings to find anything that could be a clue. They had tried removing the branches and stripping off parts of the wood for analysis. It was all to no avail. Nothing had given them any clues to his past.

"Erik, journey forth," the announcer called.

"Good luck," Tyr told him.

Erik nodded and stepped toward the first brazier as he ran his hands nervously along the side of his head.

He was alone then, even alone with his thoughts. Growing up, Tyr had always thought of Liv as his mor, but the truth had eventually surfaced about his arrival as a baby, and since she had never borne children of her own, she had taken him. Nothing could explain the amount of love Tyr had for her taking him in as her own and caring for him.

The announcer had called a handful of other young adults while he waited.

Tyr had tried to uncover any information he could through all the years, but no one in the village knew anything. Eventually he gave up asking and worked hard to become stronger and wiser so that he could uncover his past one day.

"Tyr, journey forth," the announcer called.

Today was the day he would accomplish his mission. The Warrior's Gate meant more than just becoming a Kriger; he was finally ready to start the journey into his past.

# Chapter 2: Trials of the Warriors Gate

Tyr stood tall as he walked toward the first brazier. He could see that most of the parents had gone, and a few remained a reasonable distance away, waiting for their child to arrive.

Knud stood beside the firelight. He was bald, and his beard was long and braided. He stood the same height as Tyr, and he was hunched forward. He carried a large stick to lean on and wore dark leather armor embroidered with the Kriger symbol. The symbol was a half shield, embroidered with a group of trees with the rune of courage engraved within. Extending off the right side of the shield was an axe, with the rune of faith upon the handle and the rune of ambition engraved upon the blade.

Beside Knud was a small table adorned with rune-engraved stones. "Tyr, son of Liv." Knud nodded toward Tyr as he approached the brazier.

Tyr stepped up to face Knud and gave the Kriger salute, his right hand raised over his heart, his left arm dropping to his side, then pumped his fists. "Kriger Knud," he said confidently.

Knud returned the salute, clutching the staff as he did. "I have spoken with the Seidr." He reached down and picked up three stones from the table. "There are three characteristics that every Kriger should represent. Do you remember them?"

"Yes," Tyr replied.

"Please tell me them."

"Courage, ambition, and faith."

"To accept these stones is to accept the message shared with you from the Seidr. Do you remember the prophecies the Seidr has shared with you?"

Tyr remembered. How could he forget?

The lush, green skog—forest—stood around Tyr on all sides; the trees prevented the morning sun from entering the skog. He was told to continue toward the light until he had arrived. Each step toward the light brought a different scene. The sunlight started to dim, and the mist slowly enveloped the trees. He could hear the rustle of spiders as webs began to appear in the trees around him. The small, dim light was still ahead, and he continued.

The skog was no longer lush and green. It had started to decay and wither away. Eyes of beasts could be seen through the mist, while the rustle of the wind made the branches creak and snap.

As the light faded into the mist, up ahead he could see a wooden cottage. He stepped into the clearing and saw firelight through the windows.

"Your name?" a voice called from the mist.

"Tyr," he replied and stopped in his tracks.

"Tyr…son of…Liv?" the voice called back.

"I am."

An image of an old woman appeared before the cottage. "I am Seidr. My sisters shall be along shortly."

A fire and a wooden bench appeared beside her as she stretched out her hand. "Please sit awhile, and let's begin."

Tyr approached the bench and sat. "Where am I?" he asked, glancing around.

"Tomrom." She glided through the air and settled next to him. "Though some call it the void or such nonsense."

"Is this part of the Warrior's—"

"Gate. Yes, it is. We have observed you throughout your life. To pass through the Warrior's Gate, you must receive your prophecies. These cannot be shared with anyone but yourself. To do so would dilute their power and cause your destiny to shift.

"Close your eyes a moment, child, and allow me to speak freely. It shall only be a moment, but allow the words to enter into your soul and heart."

Tyr hesitated for a moment. It was such an odd place to be, and it was unexpected. The first trial had started with him walking through the skog to end up in

Tomrom—the void? He focused upon the old woman floating in front of him. A special glow surrounded her body, and her ragged hair was scattered about her head, but her eyes were a gentle, majestic blue. Their gazes locked for a moment, then Tyr closed his eyes, and she began.

He could hear her voice humming. The woods around him started to creak and break. The wind grew in strength, circling about, and he forced himself to keep his eyes shut. He could feel the earth grumble beneath him as the dust sliced against his bare skin. Then the roaring stopped.

Moments passed. He wanted to open his eyes and forced himself not to. He could hear a gentle roar of wind around him but never felt it.

Then the humming stopped.

"Courage." Her voice was melodious.

After a moment, she continued. "Strengthened through adversity—intuition to embrace the unknown. Tough decisions lie before you—conviction in the veins. Honor shall guide your thoughts to determine right from wrong. Spoken words lead to action."

As her last word resounded, the air crackled and popped. Tyr quickly opened his eyes and shielded his ears with his hands. She was gone.

The ringing in his ears began to ease when a shade

appeared before him again, gliding softly in the air.

"My sister likes to make her exit exciting," the shade said. "I am Seidr, and my other sister shall be along shortly."

Tyr glanced up at her, shaking his head, barely able to hear her words. She looked identical to her sister, and as he glanced into her eyes, he could see that fierce, ambitious red.

"Close your eyes, Tyr, son of…Liv. Remember, do not open your eyes, or they too shall burn." The shade had started to speak another name and then corrected herself. She then waved her hand, and Tyr felt his ears and head clear.

Tyr closed his eyes.

The heat grew around him. He felt as if he was being enveloped in fire. The shade's warning was the only thing keeping his eyes shut. His body was shifting uncomfortably.

"Ambitious." Her voice was fierce. "Decisive. Competitive. No fear of the responsibility placed upon your shoulders. However, I see your heart shall become divided. You will become restless, and I know that you will sacrifice those you love most to achieve a long-lost dream."

At the last word, a freezing wind passed through his body, dousing the heat about him. He opened his eyes.

The shade was gone.

Tyr sat there in the freezing wind, which did not abate after a moment. His mind was on the words the shades had spoken. "Courage. Ambition." Whenever he thought of what they'd said, their words were there inside his mind.

"Lost in your thoughts, I see." A voice sounded about him.

Tyr looked around and saw nothing.

"Don't worry, my dear, I am here. I am Seidr, and I am the last."

"I don't see you."

"Do not fret. My sisters find it easier for you to close your eyes, but I'll allow you to keep them open. Just give me a moment."

Tyr sat still, glancing around him, trying to spot where the voice had been coming from.

Then the voice came from all directions. "Faith. Consistency. The pattern of the past shall shape the way of the future. Inner manifestations tell you what you are becoming. Without fortifications of character, all will be lost. Patience empowers your understanding."

At the last of her words, Tyr fell to the ground. The bench vanished along with the cottage, the skog lush around him once more.

Tyr sat stunned for a moment. "Faith." Things

unseen. He pushed himself off the ground and walked back to where the trial had begun. There was a lot on his mind.

Tyr returned from his thoughts and saw Knud's outstretched hand in front of him, holding the three stones. "Please accept these stones that represent the Krigere. You have passed the trial, and we hope that you always remember your meeting with the Seidr."

Tyr took the stones. Each was engraved with the runes for courage, ambition, and faith. He tightened his grip on the stones. "I will."

Knud gave him one last salute and sent him back on the path. Tyr pocketed the stones and continued toward the second brazier.

The woman stood close to the brazier, her gray hair flowing behind her head. Her back hunched forward, and her blue eyes sparkled with firelight. She smiled at him as he approached the brazier. Throughout his life, she had always given him that smile, especially during those times when he had been caught doing something he shouldn't have. Her eyes had always shown the intent behind the smile, and this one showed him that she was proud.

"Tyr, my son." Liv saluted as he stood before her.

He saluted back. "Mor Liv."

"I am proud and honored to present this necklace to you. As your mor, I am blessed by you." Then she paused, cleared her throat, and stood taller. "My son, are you looking for treasures? When you were young, you were so eager to find strength, security, and survival in your life. Look at all you have gathered." Her arms opened wide. "Your strength, security in your surroundings, and survival among us all. Tyr, you treasure life.

"This necklace depicts the Eter-Tree unfolding before you. Continue to treasure life." She spread the necklace between her hands and lifted it to Tyr.

He bent forward and let the necklace fall over his head and upon his neck. "I am blessed to have you, Mor. I will honor you by always treasuring life, as you have shown me." He then leaned forward and kissed her on the cheek.

She threw her arms around him, tears streaming down her cheeks. "My son."

They embraced each other for a moment, then Tyr started to pull away. She wrapped her arms around to keep his face level. "Treasuring life means that you and that girl need to be together. Are you together yet? She would make a great wife. I won't live forever, and I want to see you happy."

Tyr blushed and tried to pull away. "Not sure this is the right time to have that discussion."

"It's never the right time to have this discussion with you. I'm getting old, and I want to be a bestemor." She let Tyr go and gave him a shove. "Now off with you. Can't keep everyone waiting all night." She turned and walked away.

He loved Liv and knew he was blessed to have her as his mor. There wasn't anything he wouldn't do to protect her and make her happy. He turned to walk toward the third brazier while his mind was on Revna, and he knew that was precisely what Liv had intended.

The third brazier was more significant than the others and stood within the grove of trees. Beside the grove was a small hill where a large tree stood alone. The place was familiar to Tyr. Growing up, he and Revna had often met within the grove to discuss the meaning of kinship. The concept was reinforced over and over to remind them to not stand alone. To bind together to create a stronger force.

He entered the grove, glancing around, and found himself alone. He stood there in silence, remembering the stories she'd told him. The familiarity of kinship with the other children during their training had reinforced the meaning.

"You remember the story, don't you?" The familiar voice came from outside the grove.

"I do." Tyr looked up and watched a strong woman appear beside the brazier. On her left arm she carried a large wooden shield, the symbol of the Krigere engraved upon its front. The wood looked newly furnished. She held a battle-ax in her right hand. Her dark-reddish hair was pulled back into braids, and she wore her leather armor. The dents and scars of battle were shown across its front and on her skin.

She stopped and saluted. "Tyr, son of Liv."

Tyr saluted back. "Gertrude, daughter of Njal."

"What is the meaning of this grove?"

"Kinship."

"Tell me the story."

He knew the story. After the long training days, they would sit within the grove and listen to their trainers tell the story.

"'As we searched for wood,'" Tyr began, "'my child called out to me, saying, "Look at this gigantic tree. It would make a lot of good lumber, wouldn't it?"

"'No, child,' I said, 'that tree stands alone. It would not make a lot of good lumber. It would make a lot of lumber, but not good lumber. When the tree grows off by itself, too many branches grow on it. Those branches produce knots when the tree is cut into lumber. The best lumber comes from trees that grow together in groves. The trees also grow taller and straighter when they grow together.

"'So it is with us, the Krigere. We become better

individuals, more useful timber, when we grow together rather than alone.

"'Let us grow together.'"

As Tyr finished retelling the story, Gertrude had stepped forward. "I present these tokens of kinship to you." She held out the shield to Tyr. "This shield was carved from the best lumber in this grove. Let it be a reminder of your kinship with the Krigere."

Tyr accepted the shield.

"This battle-ax has been carved from the best lumber from this grove and branded with the rune of kinship. Now let it act as a reminder to use it wisely in defense of your loved ones." She presented the axe, its handle toward him, and he accepted it.

"Now let us grow together, Tyr, son of Liv." Gertrude saluted.

Tyr saluted back and watched as Gertrude turned and left the grove. He glanced down at the axe and shield in his hands and was amazed at the quality of craftsmanship. He swung them around for a moment, feeling honored to receive such gifts such as these, and then continued toward the fourth brazier.

During his walk toward the fourth brazier, the snow drifted in. The light crystal flakes fell between the flames cast from the brazier and melted into a light mist. The cold had rushed in, and Tyr shivered as it hit him. He moved closer to feel the warmth of the fourth brazier.

It stood near the well in town. Many times Tyr had rushed past the villagers gathering water at this place. He had caused more than his share of mischief when they had lost their water, when he bumped into them or knocked the buckets from their hands, only for them to have to go back and fetch another bucket from the well. He stepped away from the fire, closer to the well, and glanced down at the snow falling into its depths. He'd spent many late evenings here with Revna. It had become their place to study the history and characteristics of the Kriger people and just to talk.

Revna had disappeared for a few months at a time during other training routines. He had found himself alone at the well many times, wishing she were there with him.

A light crunch sounded behind him, and he quickly looked up. A large man was sneaking toward him, aiming an axe right at him.

Tyr rolled off the well's edge and onto his shield arm just before the axe slammed into the well. The branches on Tyr's arm helped alleviate the blow as he pushed off the ground to correct the fall and landed on his feet, his shield up in defense. He pulled the axe from the sheath on his shield.

The man smiled as they locked eyes. "Do you fear death?"

Tyr remained in the defensive stance. "I do not fear death." It was Njal, the Kriger chieftain. He stood a head taller than Tyr and had broad shoulders. Njal wore leather armor with the symbol of the Krigere showing bright in the firelight. Metal was woven into the fabric of his shoulder pads, making him look intimidating. His graying black hair blew in the cold, snowy wind, and his eyes were filled with determination.

Njal brought his axe into both hands. "Good. Then don't be afraid to run toward danger. The first to draw blood tonight wins." Njal rushed forward, slamming his axe downward.

Tyr brought his shield at an angle to meet the axe. The axe slammed against the shield, and Tyr pushed it to the side. Njal then threw his body against Tyr. Tyr was knocked off his feet and rolled to the side as he fell to the ground. Njal had brought the axe back around, and it hit the ground where Tyr had fallen. But Tyr's roll had moved him quickly out of harm's way, and now he rolled onto his knees, his stance at the ready. Njal recovered from his axe hitting the ground and brought it hard to his left. Tyr saw the incoming attack and shifted his weight onto his shield arm, ducking below the axe, and pushed the shield up. He brought his axe toward Njal's leg as he deflected. The axe skipped off the top of his shield, throwing Njal off balance as Tyr's axe connected with his leg. Tyr slowed his axe arm as it connected so that he only sliced a thin line on Njal's leg as Tyr leaped over him. Njal brought his axe around, ready for another strike against Tyr. Tyr had moved his body to face Njal and rose to his feet, his stance at the ready.

"It's over," Tyr said as Njal advanced for another strike.

"Where?"

"Your leg."

Njal glanced down and saw the small streak of blood on his leg. "Didn't even feel that happen." He lowered his axe and saluted Tyr. "Tyr, son of Liv."

"Njal, chieftain." Tyr saluted back, lowering his weapon.

"Truly you do not fear death. A Kriger through and through. It has been an honor watching you grow up to be such a fine warrior. We are blessed to have you in our village."

"The honor is all mine," Tyr responded.

Njal nodded. "I offer you this token that you may fear not death." He produced a stone from his pouch and handed it to Tyr. It had runes carved into it: *fear* and *death*. "Remember that after you have suffered through much trouble, then will the blessings come. If you fear death, you will never endure to the end. Do not allow the fear of death to bind you."

Njal saluted once more. "Tyr, you have passed the trial. Continue your journey." He started to turn and walk away. "Let's keep it our little secret that you struck first."

Tyr saluted back and nodded. He slid the stone into his pouch along with the others. "Will do."

Tyr turned and started toward the fifth brazier. Strong confidence burned within his heart. He had just struck the chieftain of the village and was asked to keep it a secret. He guessed he was the only one to do so during these trials.

Tyr held his shield and axe in his left hand as he stepped up to the fifth brazier, the most intimidating of them all. Two long tables stood beside the brazier; Tyr shook his head as he approached. Dread filled his heart as he made eye contact with Sif, the wife of the chieftain.

She stood firm before him, her height level with his own. Her red hair flowed behind her, and her eyes held wisdom and knowledge. Tyr knew what it meant to be in her presence. The tables were lined with books, scrolls, and maps. His head started to spin. The fighting he could deal with. But books meant sitting and trying to figure out what they were all talking about.

"Tyr, son of Liv." She saluted.

"Sif, wife of Njal." He saluted, trying to hide his dread of reading.

"One of the most important characteristics of the Kriger is the relentless pursuit of knowledge. This hasn't been your strongest characteristic, but through your struggles you have overcome this and shown, or rather accepted, that constant knowledge shall be for your good." She was a soft-spoken woman, and she knew that he hated—dreaded—reading, and that hands-on learning had always been better for him. Taking up a weapon and defending himself was superior to picking up a book and debating the topics therein.

"You always pushed me to better myself. To not give up when it got tough." Tyr glanced around at the tables. "We aren't reading tonight, are we?"

She laughed. "No. Tonight I award you with this token." She lifted a stone with the rune for learning etched into it.

He accepted the stone and slid it in with the others. "Thank you." He let his breath out in relief.

"When we have knowledge of the world around us,

we can use that knowledge to build and protect our families. Do you remember what knowledge trains you in?"

He quickly looked up as if to glance into his mind. "Self-denial and…self-mastery."

"Perfect. Knowledge is that which you cannot give to others, but it can be used to guide. Only you can pay the price it takes to study and to develop your talents, Tyr, son of Liv. This token shall remind you that you should continue to seek and absorb knowledge to acquire the necessary skills."

Tyr nodded in agreement. "Sif, there has been no greater teacher than you. I am grateful for the opportunity to have learned from such a wise and learned person as yourself." He bowed his head then. "Thank you."

She acknowledged him with a bow of her own head and continued. "Do not let your pursuit of knowledge destroy you. Remember what we have taught you about the Voktere and how…"

Tyr let his mind wander at that point. The word Voktere made him remember conversations with his friends.

One night near the well, he recalled, he and his friends had been discussing their lesson on the Voktere from earlier that day.

"They can't be all that bad," Erik had said.

"Have you ever met one before?" Revna asked.

"No…no, it's just the way people talk about them all being evil," Erik said. "Just feels so absolute. They can't all be that bad. Maybe we just have it all wrong about them. What do you think, Tyr?"

Tyr had been gazing into the distance when he heard Erik's question. He had the same thoughts as Erik on the topic. He knew in his heart that there was no way every Vokter could be evil. However, the lessons had taught them differently. "I know what you mean, Erik. We'll never truly know until we have the chance to meet a Vokter. But according to our history lessons, they were all wiped out."

"They are wrong," Erik blurted out. "Don't you remember when we were out on training missions, and I swore I saw one? It was on the ridge, but I saw it."

"Not this again," Revna cut in. "Erik, it was the northern lights messing with your eyes."

"You were there!"

"Let's not discuss what you saw anymore. I just can't wait for the Warrior's Gate trials to be over so I can get on with my life." Revna walked over to the well. "If the history books were wrong, Erik, then maybe one day we'll get the chance to judge the Voktere for ourselves." She glanced down into the well as she spoke.

"I…you're right." Erik walked over to the well. "I hope that we do get that chance to meet one and to find out the history books were wrong."

Tyr remained quiet as they continued to talk. The books had intrigued him whenever they described the Voktere. How they had tethered themselves to the spirits of the beasts of the land. Though the stories all ended in bloodshed, Tyr still believed there had to be some good that had come from the Voktere…

Sif clapped loudly in front of Tyr's face. "Off dreaming again?" she shouted.

Tyr shook his head and remembered where he was. "I guess."

"What was it this time?" Sif rocked back on her heels. "Sea voyages? Saving a young maiden in need? The awesome way your shadow looks during weapon practice?"

"No, the Voktere."

"Oh. It wasn't off topic then. Remember our warnings and what history has shown us about the Voktere. The stories will protect us as long as we heed them." She laid her hand on his shoulder. "Tyr, continue on the path you are on, and constantly seek knowledge. The last step of the Warrior's Gate is just up ahead. I ask you to promise to never share this knowledge of the Warrior's Gate with anyone once you have passed through the last trial. Once you salute, you are under oath to keep these details secret so as to allow the others to embark on their own journeys." She stepped back and saluted him.

Tyr saluted back. He committed to the oath. Then he stepped away, heading toward the last brazier.


The last brazier sat at the village entrance. A tall wooden barrier that surrounded the village stood firm beyond the firelight. The gate stood roughly two men high; smaller wooden platforms within the walls allowed the guards to step up to the wall to stand watch. There were four guards posted, two on either side. Stationed every twenty yards was another post with its guard, surrounding the entire perimeter of the village.

Tyr approached the hilltop to see the barrier standing in the distance, along with large groups of people standing beyond the brazier. A wooden archway stood erect just beyond the brazier. It stood right before smaller braziers stationed around the groups, causing shadows to dance against the wooden arch and barrier beyond. Snow skittered through the air, cast about in the wind. A light dusting of snow covered the ground; the snowfall had begun to slow.

"Tyr, son of Liv," boomed a voice from beyond the brazier. "He has passed through the Warrior's Gate as one of our own. Welcome, Kriger Tyr. Proceed through the gate."

The cheers, clapping, and yelling roared beyond the brazier as the announcer finished his words. Tyr stepped forward, hearing his name being chanted. He found his friends beyond the gate; each carried a shield and axe identical to his own. Beyond the gate stood Liv, his adopted mor, tears streaming down her face as she smiled and cheered for him. He stepped through the gate and hugged her.

"Everyone is so proud of you." She embraced him, and he hugged her tight. They stood like that for a few moments, then she spoke. "Enjoy the festivities and remember what I told you earlier: I won't live forever." She winked and nodded toward Revna. "Go, be with your friends."

"Thanks, Mor." He blushed.

Tyr rushed over to his friends.

"Congratulations, you two!" he said as he arrived by their sides. "Those are some cool-looking shields."

"Would be even cooler if Njal hadn't knocked a big chunk from the side of it." Erik lifted his shield, showing that a piece was missing on the side. "Brand new, then he breaks it the same night."

"Mine is perfect." Revna lifted hers. "He didn't even get close. Nicked his arm before he could get near me."

"You hit him?" Tyr questioned.

Erik and Revna just stared at him. Then Revna said, "Yeah…didn't you?"

"Well, yeah." Tyr tried to act confident.

"I don't think Njal was trying all that hard," Erik said. "It took a while for me to get an opening, but I eventually found it. I think he wanted to see how much fear we'd show if death was on the line. Though he pulled his strikes as much as he could."

Tyr just stood there astonished. Njal hadn't cared to keep it a secret. He would have killed Tyr if he had been trying. He thought back to the fight and the techniques Njal had used. They'd felt genuine to him, but now he knew that Njal had been messing with him all along. His confidence boost from earlier drifted away.

Cheering erupted to the sides as another young one completed the Warrior's Gate trial. They looked up and saw the newest member of the Kriger community step through the Warrior's Gate to be greeted by his family.

"Wish I was first, Revna. I would have been there waiting for you to pass through," Tyr said as he turned back to his friends.

"It's fine. Liv was there for me, and she made sure I

knew that I was loved."

Of course Liv had been there. Revna and Tyr had always been together since they were young. When Revna's mor had passed away, Liv had been there, not only for Tyr but also for Revna. "That's good."

They stood there exchanging stories of the Warrior's Gate and how they had endured it. Erik said Gertrude was distraught that he had forgotten most of the kinship story.

Revna had received her mor's necklace from Liv during the treasured life trial. She thought it had been lost for years, but Liv was able to track it down and had saved it for today. Revna's eyes misted up when she retold the story.

After the last of the new Krigere had completed the Warrior's Gate, Njal came before the final brazier and raised his hand in a gesture to be heard. Everyone tapped each other until the crowd was silent and focused upon him.

"Dream big and work hard. That is what you have accomplished today. When you were children in the village, it may have been your dream to become a Kriger. That dream may have felt big at the time, but you worked hard at it. You have learned our ways, and now you are the generation to inspire the next.

"Do not forget the bond you have forged here today.

All of you have completed the Warrior's Gate and become Krigere."

Cheers rose from the crowd. Tyr and his friends joined in.

Njal raised his hand once more. The crowd fell silent. "Enjoy the festivities!"

The crowd cheered again, then went back to their discussions. Others came from around the village. Carts loaded with food pulled into the area, and activities began around them. Music started playing to allow for dancing.

"Excuse me." A child tapped Tyr on the leg. Tyr glanced down and found two of his favorite children looking up at him.

He knelt. "How are you doing, Berner and Elsie?"

"We came here to celebrate with you! We want to be just like you when we grow up," Elsie said.

"Can I hold your axe?" Berner asked.

Tyr pulled his axe from his shield arm and handed it to Berner. "Don't hurt yourself with that thing."

"I want the shield!" Elsie exclaimed.

He handed her the shield, and they took off running. Elsie could barely hold the shield out in front of her. "I am Kriger Tyr, fear me!" she shouted.

"I am Tyr. You can be Revna," Berner called out, hefting the axe as best he could.

"At least one of them wants to be you, Revna," Tyr said. "I was worried they were going to want to play Erik. He always dies when they play him." Tyr looked over at Revna, and Erik punched him in the arm.

Tyr enjoyed the company of his friends. They ate with each other, and then he had to pry his shield and axe from Berner and Elsie when their parents took them home. Tyr's life was full of joy, good friends, and family, and he had the opportunity to dance with Revna before the night came to an end.

The snow continued to fall gradually throughout the night. That joy wasn't going to last long.

# Chapter 3: The Spion

The following day, Tyr awoke to the deep, loud calls of war horns. The horns were used to warn of danger.

He quickly rolled out of his bed as the door to his room was thrown open. He turned to engage the intruder.

"Tyr!" Erik yelled as he moved out of the way of Tyr's fist and pushed Tyr against the wall. "What are you doing? And why don't you have a shirt on?"

"I just woke up!" Tyr shoved off the wall. "I always sleep without a shirt. It gets caught in on this." He waved at the branches on his arm.

Erik was dressed in his war equipment, war horn at his side. He looked in a hurry, with the Kriger leather armor and shield, his axe in his left hand. "Uh…doesn't matter. Get dressed. We're at war."

Tyr started digging through his room. Clothes were thrown everywhere, reading material was left open, and he had left the dessert last night out on his bed. He found his armor under a pile of dirty clothes and started tossing things around to get to his equipment. He needed to find his war horn. "What's happening?" he asked as he dressed and continued to toss things about.

"The front gate was destroyed, the guards dead. It

happened before anyone could sound the alarm. Njal took a handful of Krigere to chase down the intruders. He has the others watching the villagers." His voice was panicked.

Tyr could see the sweat on his brow. Erik was scared. He finished lacing up the leather armor, then lifted his new shield and axe. "Can't find my war horn—we'll just use yours. What are our orders?"

"We're to head out to help Njal and the others." Erik started through the door, Tyr close behind. "He wanted us to go around the other direction in case they decided to come back."

Liv was nowhere to be found as they left the house. Six inches of snow had covered the village during the night. Tracks were imprinted across the whole village and then led out into the snow. On their approach to the gate, he could see crimson snow below the platforms. Two guards hung limp against the railing. Two others lay near the gate. The wooden doors were knocked inward, and large chunks of wood lay across the snow. Armed Krigere ordered families back to their homes.

Tyr looked at the bodies of those with whom he had just spent the night in celebration.

"Get back to your post!" a Kriger said harshly to them. The horns blared again in warning.

"We're set to rendezvous with the others," Erik said, and his voice had a nervous tic. He waved to Tyr and himself. "We're to go together."

"Get out there and bring us honor." The Kriger saluted, then went back to his duties. He approached a family walking toward one of the guards lying in crimson snow. "Get back to your homes."

"Is that…oh no." The woman stared at the guard's body, then started to sob. "I am…his…wife."

The voices died away as Tyr and Erik left the village behind them and found the tracks leading east toward the skog. "We should bring Revna with us. She is a better tracker than both of us," Tyr mentioned as they examined the tracks.

"No time for that. She has her orders, we have ours." Erik examined the tracks too. "We're going to circle to the north. Let's go."

They quickened their steps, heading north away from the skog. A war horn came from the skog to the east. Tyr stopped and looked toward it. "We should go in here."

Erik was up ahead of Tyr and shook his head. "Not yet."

They continued north for a bit. Tyr wondered why they were going so far away from the village. The war horns came from the skog once more but from farther south. They had trained over the years, and he knew the others were circling about within the skog to trap the intruders. The war horn helped pinpoint their location to allow the others to circle back in. However, he and Erik were heading north without circling back at all. He stopped again. "We trained together, Erik. We should go in here, and you know it." Tyr stepped forward, and his anger started to rise.

"Just a little further, then we'll head back around. We need to be sure…Didn't you see their bodies… lying in the snow?" Erik stepped back toward Tyr. Tears came to his eyes. "Just imagine what they would do to the others if we're wrong."

He had a point, Tyr thought. If they circled back too soon, they would leave an opening for the intruders to strike again. But the other half of Tyr knew that Njal would have their hide if they didn't follow orders. He reached down to his side where his war horn should be and remembered he had left it. "You hear the horn… Sound your war horn, and let's go. Njal needs us to circle back in."

Erik looked north, then back at him. "Let's just get to that hill and see what we find. Then we'll head in, I promise." He glanced back toward the hill once more and back to Tyr. "We need to hurry. Now." And with that, Erik took off in a sprint heading north up the hill.

Tyr called for him to stop, then headed after him.

Njal wasn't going to be happy at all. Erik disappeared beyond the hilltop. Tyr huffed it up the hill steadily, then crested the hilltop and found five armed warriors on it. They stood far from one another, and he saw Erik kneeling in the snow with a crossbow to his head, his shield and axe tossed aside in the snow.

Tyr pulled his axe from his shield and went into a defensive posture. "Let him go."

"Now, now," came a voice from the center warrior. "We're just here to talk to you for a moment." He lifted his hands, showing he held no weapons. His black hair was tied in a knot with animal skin.

Tyr had no way of sounding the war horn to inform the others of his location and to use certain deep tones to pass a message along. Erik had his horn, but Tyr could not reach it.

The man glanced from Tyr to Erik and found what Tyr was looking for. He walked over and pulled the horn from Erik's side. "Are you wanting to warn the others?" He lifted the horn to his lips and played the deep tones to pass the message along.

Tyr was shocked to hear the man play the correct tones in perfect pitch. "How?"

"Does it matter? We need to talk and quickly. They'll be on their way here now." The man tossed the horn into the snow and then waved to the warrior holding the crossbow to Erik's head. "Let him go."

The warrior moved the crossbow away from Erik's head and pointed it at Tyr.

Erik shuffled forward and lifted his shield and axe. He avoided looking directly at Tyr as he stood. "Is our deal complete?"

"It will be if you finish your part. Now go, my little spion," the black-haired man said.

Tyr's shock grew deeper. Anxiety set in as he watched Erik turn to walk away. "Spion…Erik, what is happening? Talk to me, Erik!" Then despair set in. "We were brothers."

Erik never glanced back at Tyr. He ran back down the hill toward the village.

"We're in a bit of a hurry," the man said. "But first, introductions are in order. I am Gorm, and we already know who you are—Tyr." Gorm bowed. His green eyes were focused on Tyr the entire time.

# Chapter 4: A Gorm Assault

Tyr felt despair cascading through his body. The shock and betrayal of his friend had just begun to sink in while being surrounded by five warriors. He focused his attention on the man pointing the crossbow at him. The only one holding any weapon at the moment was him. Tyr shifted his breathing. He couldn't allow fear to take over his thinking. Betrayed. Alone. The last word had been there most of his life, and it wasn't going to stop today.

The breathing heated his blood, and his emotions boiled into a deep-drawn rage. The odds were against him, and it fueled the flames.

*Do not fear death.* Njal's words rushed through his mind as he charged toward the man holding the crossbow. When the crossbow went off, Tyr had his shield drawn and ready. The bolt struck the strong wood and barely pierced it. Tyr brought his axe toward the crossbow, knocking it from the man's hand, then followed through, throwing his shield into the man's face.

The man fell backward into the snow, knocked out cold. Tyr spun to engage the others. They had backstepped in front of Gorm, their weapons all drawn.

Controlling the rage would allow Tyr to focus on his

opponents. He had gone through rigorous training to harness the skill. He had the advantage of surprise. They were all ready for what was coming next.

Tyr rushed toward the outermost warrior. The warrior's sword arced wide; Tyr slipped under the blade, letting the weapon slam against the branches on his arm and bringing his shield upward. The sword went wide, and the shield slammed against his chin, throwing him backward. Tyr had been focused on the next warrior as his shield connected. His axe slammed against the sword, sending it wide. He brought his shield forward to block the next strike. Tyr got the bottom of the axe against the attacker's arm and pulled the warrior to the ground, leaving a long gash where the axe had connected.

He glanced up in time to see a foot flying toward his chest; he hadn't had time to dodge. It connected and knocked him back. As his back hit the snow, he rolled backward to gain ground.

The warrior who had kicked him, along with Gorm, had stopped advancing and stepped back. The other three warriors lay in the snow, the last one grabbing his arm to stop the rush of blood. The snow melted where the blood made its new home.

"Won't be enough," Gorm said.

"The odds…aren't against me…anymore," Tyr said as he steadied his breathing.

"So sure of yourself. Typical Kriger." Gorm thrust his arm forward, and a light appeared on the scales upon his arm. Then a giant spirit serpent appeared in the snow. Its eyes were those of thunder. The serpent's scales were covered in spiritual light, and it slithered through the snow. It slid past the two men and was visible above their bodies.

The other warrior had made no movement, and runes appeared on the pelt he wore. A wolf appeared in the snow beside him; it was identical to the ones found in the area. Its fur stood on end, and its body was a translucent spirit with a glow surrounding it.

Tyr had never seen it done like this before. The stories, those told to him repeatedly, had mentioned the spiritual creatures that could be called upon. He felt his defensive posture waning as he watched the creatures, then caught himself. He stepped back, unsure what would happen next.

"Figured it out yet?" Gorm mused.

Tyr glanced between the serpent and wolf. "Voktere."

"Taking my warriors down was one trick, but these are entirely different," Gorm said. As if on cue, the wolf rushed forward and leaped.

Tyr brought his shield to block the approaching wolf and saw the serpent shoot forward through the snow.

He pushed his shield against the wolf and stepped backward away from the approaching serpent, sending his axe toward its massive body. The serpent slid around the axe as it slammed into the snow, and the wolf quickly recovered and brought its teeth to bear against his leg. Pain erupted into his mind. He then harnessed the rage and swung the shield down hard against the wolf's neck. It howled and let go of his leg as it evaporated into the air as if it were never there. The serpent had wound itself around his body. He brought his axe down against its scales, and it slithered on around his body. It was quick, and it tore the axe from his hands and cast it aside. His body was engulfed by the giant serpent, and his shield slipped to the snow below. His body was raised off the ground as the serpent brought its face before Tyr, its thunderous eyes focused intently on his. Then it lowered him to his feet, its body slowly increasing the pressure against his body.

"Have you heard of the Jormungandr, the giant sea serpent? This is one of its many spawn." Gorm stood beside the serpent and stroked the top of its head. "Fylgjur, we call them. I presume that you haven't heard the name before."

"Can't—breathe—" Tyr felt the breath leaving his body as the serpent continued to tighten.

"As I said before, we're in a bit of a hurry." Gorm pulled a vial from his pouch, dipped a sharp quill into it, and passed the vial to the last standing warrior. "Should be quick." He then thrust the quill into the left side of Tyr's neck. "These serpents are hard to find and even harder to kill. They can shock their prey."

Tyr felt his body convulse as the serpent pulsed. The serpent paused and pulsed a handful of times.

"The shock will cause your body to focus upon your heart, and with the poison I've given you, it will be only a matter of time before it stops."

"What do you—" Tyr couldn't finish the sentence. His mind wasn't able to focus much as he spoke. He was only able to force a few words out.

"Want?" Gorm patted the serpent on the head, and the pulsing stopped. "You're stronger than I would have given you credit for, but that is beside the point. Blowing the horn was part of the plan to draw the warriors here. With them distracted by your death, we'll gather the hostages needed to get what we want. We have been looking for a relic, and it just so happens to be in your possession."

A relic? Hostages? Tyr hadn't even seen any stone besides the ones given to him throughout the trial the day before, and none of the stones he possessed had any particular value to him. He didn't want any harm to come to anyone in the village. "You can…have it. Just leave…the others alone," he said, catching his breath. He could feel the toxins moving down his neck and arm.

"That's the problem. We haven't found it. We've looked through all of your possessions and found nothing resembling the relic." He walked over to Tyr's left side and tapped the branches on his arm. "Even these branches in your arm were not what we needed. We'll go with the hostages and leave a message to bring the relic to us in the abandoned Kriger village, Eski. Northeast of here. Your chieftain knows it well and will get what we need to save his people.

"And the best part is that death brings it all about. The relic won't appear among your possessions until your death. My spion will find it, and poor old Njal won't have what he needs to save his people. Either way, my spion will show at Eski unless Njal brings us what we need."

Tyr couldn't understand how his death had anything to do with the relic. "Let me go. I'll help you find what you need. Just leave the others alone."

Gorm tapped the serpent on the head, and its eyes filled with lightning and sparked. "This is the only way."

Tyr tried to focus as the pain rushed through his body as the serpent continued. Betrayed by his friend, he had finally met a Vokter and wouldn't live to share it with Revna. Oh, Revna! How his heart ached then, and he couldn't tell if it was his longing to see her once more or the toxins in his blood. How could it end like this?

He hadn't said goodbye to those he loved. Hadn't thanked Liv for being the mor he'd never had, hadn't told her how grateful he was. He focused on the previous day and all the joy he had felt celebrating with those he loved.

Then he faded into darkness.

# Chapter 5: The Relic

"*Fornyelse. Vakne, Tyr.*" The voice was melodious. He could feel the warmth throughout his body as the voice spoke, particularly in his left shoulder. "*Fornyelse. Tyr, vakne!*" The voice rose to a crescendo, and he could feel his body shaking in the cold wind against his face.

Tyr's eyes widened to find snow falling from the sky and the outline of a woman shaking him.

"He is awake!" the woman yelled as she saw his eyes open. Tyr couldn't make sense of what they were all saying. He was dazed and groggy, and the voices were muffled.

"—him up out of the—" He heard a man's voice.

Someone started pulling him out of the snow. When he was settled into a seated position, he blinked several times and felt as if he had been dunked in a bath of ice.

"—happened—?" He could see the man approaching.

Then red lit his eyes as he felt a hand across his face. He blinked again and felt the rush throughout his body. It was Gertrude and Njal.

"What happened?" Njal asked.

"Erik…Voktere…" His mind raced through the events, and he found himself speaking in one-word sentences. He couldn't form the words that he needed.

Then he remembered the hostages. "Hostages…We— the village. They are…in trouble. Gorm…"

"Gorm!" Njal placed his hands on Tyr's face, forcing him to look him in the eyes. "You aren't making any sense. How do you know that name?"

"Far, give him a moment." Gertrude pulled Njal's hands away from Tyr's face. "Here, drink this." She lifted a skin of water, and he drank.

Njal kicked the snow. "We need answers!"

Tyr shook his head, trying to clear his mind and relay the information. "We need…to get back."

At those words, a war horn blew from the south, and smoke started to fill the sky over the hilltop.

"No." Njal's voice broke. "Gertrude, leave him. Odger bring Tyr back to the village. We leave now." He broke into a sprint and leaped over the hilltop down toward the village, Gertrude right behind.

An older man approached, steadying him. "Tyr, it's me, Odger," he said. "Finish drinking. You're going to need it." His eyes drifted from Tyr to where the smoke rose from the south. The village of Kjarra was burning.

The men Tyr had knocked into the snow were gone and only had left blood behind. Gorm must have taken them with him when he left.

Odger had applied a salve to Tyr's leg and neck and covered it with moss. Then he helped Tyr gather his things. They headed down the hill and back toward the burning village. They passed through the splintered gates and found homes burning. The grove of trees blazed in a firestorm, and the giant tree upon the hill burned alone.

There was no commotion of fighting, no harsh words being spoken, only mourning and the hurried voices of those carrying buckets from the well and lake below to douse the flames.

A small group of women and children huddled near the gates. A few more of their kin had been slain. Krigere were lifting the bodies of their fallen and placing them beside each other near the gate walls.

Tyr hadn't returned to full strength, but with the aid of Odger, he had been able to recover. Sorrow entered his heart as he saw his village burning and his kin mourning.

"Will you be fine from here?" Odger asked.

"Yes, thank you, Odger," Tyr responded.

Odger went to help douse the flames.

Tyr walked over to the bodies. None of them were Revna, Erik, or Liv. He rushed to his house, and the door was bashed in. Everything was torn apart. His home was in shambles. In the small living area, the table had been turned over, the chairs smashed, the pelts they lay on thrown on the floor, and manuscripts, papers, and decorations tossed about. He stepped over the broken wood and toward the living quarters. He found the doors splintered in. He looked into his mor's room. The pelt she lay on was tossed on the floor, papers and books were torn apart, and her clothes were tossed to and fro. Liv was nowhere to be found.

He turned and looked into his room. It was a mess, even messier than he had left it. Clothes had been tossed into a pile across the room. His belongings had all been opened and strewn about. His blanket was ripped and covered in mud. His favorite readings were torn apart and thrown about.

He couldn't take it and turned to leave. He rushed out of his home and into the cold open air, where the snow was falling steadily.

The smoke and ash made the snow an ashen black on the ground. It started to create a thin layer upon the whiteness of the snow.

Tyr's world was upside down. He couldn't understand how Erik had betrayed him. Even the thought of Erik's name made his anger rise. He was going to get to the bottom of it, and Erik would pay.

He started to remember what had happened. His death was needed—the relic, what was it? He had never seen anything remarkable in his possession. He would figure out what they had been after, but first, he needed to find Erik.

He found the fires dying down, and the Krigere had stopped carrying the fallen to be lined up with the others. Then he found Njal near the gates, and their eyes met.

"Now would be a good time to talk, boy!" He ran toward Tyr.

Gertrude stepped in front of him and shoved him. "Far, wait!" But she fell onto her rump, and Njal's charge never slowed.

Tyr lifted his hands in submission. He let the shield slip from his left hand and lie in the snow.

Njal slowed and grabbed Tyr by the front of his shirt, heaving him off his feet. "Talk!"

Tyr recounted the story, and Njal let him go.

"Erik, a spion? No. Has anyone seen or found Erik's body?" he asked the crowd of Krigere gathering around them.

They shook their heads.

"Have we found all the dead? Who else are we missing?" Njal asked.

One Kriger spoke up. "More than a dozen are missing, including women, children, and a few of the Krigere. The dead have all been accounted for."

"What happened here?" Njal's voice started to rise.

"We were unable to stop them," the Kriger said. "They had creatures with them, and no matter how many times we killed them, they appeared with more of these creatures. Wolves, serpents, bears, ravens, and trolls. We were distracted at the gates, being overwhelmed. Then the grove started to burn behind us. We dispatched the remaining ethereal beasts and hunted down others within the village. Then they were gone, and we dared not follow them into the skog."

Njal looked down for a moment. "Voktere. The same that Tyr encountered, and with Gorm leading them."

"We did find this note upon one of the bodies." Sune, one of the newest Krigere, approached holding a parchment and handed it to Njal, who read it quickly.

"Huglausi!" Njal crumpled the paper in his hands. "They took hostages and ran with their tails between their legs! What is this relic they speak of? You mentioned it but didn't know what it was."

Tyr had told them everything down to the last detail, except Gorm's assertion that Tyr's death would bring about the relic's existence. He hadn't died, and now the hostages were going to die. Without the relic, Gorm was never going to let them go. Tyr's house had been searched, his belongings tossed about. Erik was nowhere to be found. They must have found the relic.

"I have no relic and know nothing about it," Tyr replied. "My house was ransacked, and my mor is missing. They must have found what they were looking for and taken the hostages anyway."

"Odger, prepare for war," Njal said. "We march upon Eski in the morning. And prepare the bodies for a proper burial. Gertrude, search Tyr's belongings for the relic. Take Sune with you. Tyr, you don't move until Gertrude has completed her search, I'm going to find Erik and get some answers." He stalked off down toward the well.

Tyr had wanted to ask him about Gorm, but it hadn't been the time with so many others around. He watched as the Krigere moved about as ordered. Gertrude pushed past him and entered his home, stepping upon the broken door as she went. Sune followed. He could hear his house being torn apart even more, and he had to step away.

He walked over to the bodies, examining them. Liv, Revna, and Erik weren't there. But he found other faces that were hard to see after the joy at the Warrior's Gate celebration. He saw the dad of Elsie and Berner, the young children he had played with the night before. Their far had been the blacksmith of the village, working day and night to produce quality weapons for the Kriger arsenal. Tyr turned away from the bodies to find the children.

He approached the women and children but couldn't spot Elsie and Berner, or his mor. "Have you seen Liv, Elsie, or Berner?" he asked one of the women.

"No…they must have been taken with the others."

She had tears in her eyes. "Taken."

His heart sank; they hadn't been found. He couldn't sit around waiting for the searchers to find them. He took off running through the village, calling for them.

Hours passed by as his search continued in vain. He found no trace of any of them. All those closest to him had been taken—Revna, Erik, Liv, Berner, and Elsie, and who knew who else. He balled his hands into fists as he fell back against the walls of his house. He slammed his fists into the snow and tossed it about, then dropped his face into his hands and yelled.

Stillness followed, and he watched as the bodies were piled into wagons and taken to the burial grounds. Families opened their doors to those who had lost their homes.

One of the women brought him a plate of food and drink, and he gave her his thanks. She nodded and returned to provide others with food and drink.

Gertrude had concluded her search with nothing in hand, and Tyr watched Knud return from talking with Njal at the well.

"Tyr, we haven't found Erik or Liv, or any trace of them. We sent a search party into the skog to search for any others, but they were instructed not to go far," Knud said.

"Any sign of Revna?" Tyr asked.

"No."

"They have to be out there somewhere." Tyr closed his eyes, remembering seeing Revna and Liv the night before.

"We'll find them." Knud then cleared his throat. "Your orders are to stand down and stay in the village until we return with the hostages."

"I'm going!"

"Njal doesn't want you near any of this. Tyr, my boy, he doesn't believe anything you have told him. Not without Erik, this relic, or anything else to go on besides the note."

"Half-troll," Tyr said under his breath. "I need to go! Gorm is going to kill them without the relic."

"I don't know how you came to know that name, but please stop using it." Knud winced, and his voice came out hard. "Njal has chosen to allow you to remain unchained here in the village to protect those left behind. Speak that name to him or anyone else, though, and he'll throw you in chains."

"But—"

"Leave it at that. Eski is a couple of days' journey from here. It will all be over soon, one way or another," Knud said and walked back toward the well.

Tyr slammed his head back against his home, closing his eyes. Tyr had never given Njal any reason to think he would lie, and now he was being accused of it without witnesses. Where had the men he fought on the hilltop gone? They had engaged in combat against the Voktere, and Njal chose to ignore it all. The Krigere in the village had to have gotten through to Njal after encountering the ethereal creatures, Tyr thought. Ignorance would be their downfall at this point.

He sat with his thoughts, going over the encounter with Erik and Gorm and wondering why he hadn't died. He had been sure he was going to die when he was wrapped in the serpent's scales, along with the poison in his neck.

Tyr opened his eyes when he heard a rustle come from within his house. He pushed off the ground, lifting his shield and axe, and moved quickly and quietly. He tried to step over the ground without making a sound but couldn't help the cracking of broken wood beneath his feet. The sound was coming from his room. He rushed forward, his shield before him, and found the intruder.

They knelt upon the mess on the floor and scattered papers and clothes about.

"Revna?" Tyr lowered his shield. "What are you doing in here?"

"Tyr!" She leaped off the floor and threw her arms around him. "I thought you were dead."

Her arms around his neck broke him down. After all that had happened, he threw his arms around her, and tears streamed down his face. His shield and axe dropped instantly to the floor. "I thought *you* were dead."

They held each other for a moment, then Revna stepped back. "Why would I be dead? You know I'm the best here." She wiped tears from her eyes.

"No one could find you or my mor. Or Erik." The last words came out harder than he had wanted.

"Erik and I were out in the skog chasing them down. They had taken Liv, his parents, and even the little ones. Erik disappeared after the ones carrying his little sister, but we never saw him again. They got away." Revna kicked at the trash on the ground. "When I got back, I saw them hauling the bodies to the burial and couldn't bear to see if you were among them. Then I heard Gertrude telling Njal she hadn't found some relic they needed to get the hostages back, and I rushed over here." Tears filled her eyes.

"I'm okay," Tyr reassured her, reaching out to touch her shoulder.

"I know that now." She wiped at the tears. "When I got here, I just started to throw things around, hoping to find this relic in hopes that I could bring Liv home. She is the last family I have."

Tyr choked back tears. "She is the only family I've got too. Let me help you."

He knelt and started to push things around the room, looking for anything that could be the relic. Revna knelt and began to go through things.

Tyr rummaged through the clothes and found a wooden box. It was smashed, the wood barely holding together. He lifted the broken lid off and started to pull out a few items.

"Liv said this box was with me when she found me. It contained money, a note with my name inscribed on it, and a message to whoever found me." He pulled out a ripped paper, now smudged.

"You've shown me that before. Do you still have the book that came with it?" Revna looked over his shoulder into the box.

"It isn't in here. Probably someone took it or tossed it." He waved his hands around the room. "It's kind of a mess."

She laughed. "Let's keep looking."

He lay on the ground, looking under his cot, and pushed clothes and trash away. Then he spotted the book. He groaned and shoved his body under the cot to reach it. He pulled himself out and held the book up. "Found it."

"Isn't it empty, though?" Revna asked.

"Yeah, the book has nothing in it." He opened the book and flipped through the pages. Nothing was scrawled upon the blank parchment. "Nothing." He closed the book with his left hand and felt it crack in his grasp.

Tyr tried to drop the book and move away from it, but it clung to his skin. It transformed into a wooden spiderlike creature, and he tried to shake it off. "Revna!"

She turned and saw the wooden spider crawl around to the top of Tyr's hand. The pages turned into spines along its back and shot into his hand. Tyr screamed in pain.

Revna grabbed the spider and tried yanking it away. It continued to bury itself in the top of Tyr's hand.

"Get it off!" Tyr was pulling at the spines that had embedded themselves. He broke one off before another shot into his skin.

Revna broke more spines off the spider as it started to settle into his hand. In the center was a small rectangle bearing a single rune that had been inscribed on the side of the book. The pieces that formed the spider snapped off and fell to the ground, leaving only the rectangle, along with six spiked spines embedded into his hand. It then gave a faint blue glow, and Tyr felt excruciating pain.

Revna tried to pull the block off, then applied a small knife to it, but it was useless.

Tyr couldn't focus past the pain, for it was too much. He slammed his hand against the side of his cot, then lay down. "Get…Njal."

"No, you need to rest. Let me get this off of you," Revna said as she laid one hand on his head and the other upon the wood now embedded in his hand. "You're burning up."

"It burns…Can't think." Tyr rolled in agony.

"I'll—"

Before he could hear her last words, he blacked out.

# Chapter 6: Hel…Hele…

"Fornyelse." His body felt the warm, melodious voice once more. "Fornyelse."

The voice came as Tyr's surroundings changed. The darkness lifted in a haze, and light appeared around him. In front of him was a large tree surrounded by water and stones. He stepped forward from the white space onto the stones.

"Welcome, Tyr," came the voice, and a woman appeared before him. Her skin was covered in bark. Her hair fell behind her head, green and woven with leaves throughout. She was small and beautiful, her eyes were light green, her smile was heavenly. Vines wrapped her body as tightly as clothing and fell lightly at her sides.

"Am I dreaming? Where am I?" Tyr asked, looking into the vast whiteness surrounding this place.

"We are within your mind, and in my sanctuary." She waved her hand, and stone benches appeared. "Please have a seat. We'll be here awhile."

He was hesitant; the last day had worn at his trust. He viewed the surroundings and found only her. He had no weapons of his own, and his clothing was a simple shirt and leggings. He had the relic attached to his left hand, along with the branches running up his arm; the pain wasn't there. He saw that she carried no weapons, so he approached the bench slowly and sat beside her.

"Do you know who I am?" she asked; her voice was very soothing to hear. It made him feel safe and warm.

"I do not. How come I have never met or heard about you?"

"What do you know about your past?" she asked.

"Nothing." The word left his mouth before he could think. There was no information about his past before he'd arrived in Kjarra. No one had ever asked him first about his past. "What do you know?"

"A lot." She paused.

After brief moments of silence, Tyr became impatient. "What can you tell me about my past?"

"Very few details at this point."

"Then what am I doing here?"

"Tyr, your mind has suffered great trauma. I have renewed your body and started to heal your mind. It will take time for a full recovery. Until then I must keep what I share to a minimum. Fornyelse," she said and waved her hand in a circle before her. Light green tendrils flowed through the air and landed upon Tyr.

Warmth spread throughout his body, and he felt his mind clearing. "What are you doing?"

"Healing the trauma. I was awakened when you

were brought to the brink of death. I slowed the poison before it reached your heart and then started to heal your wounds."

"Awakened?"

"The relic in your hand." She gestured to it. "You called me when you put that on."

She spoke of the relic. The one they had been looking for was now embedded in Tyr's hand. "They were looking for this. Why do they want it?"

"I cannot answer that at this moment. Please give me time."

He stood up then. "They took familes away, children, women…my mor!" The whiteness started to darken around them.

"Calm your mind."

"I can't calm down! They were after this, and now I can't take it off." He pulled at it, and it wouldn't budge.

"Sit and be calm before—" she started. Then darkness began to fall around the sanctuary. "Calm…"

He could see her fading away. All of it was fading away. Then he stopped. He started to control his breathing, allowing his emotions to subside. Then it all came to the forefront of his mind. Betrayed by Erik. Poisoned and almost dead. His loved ones were taken, and there was nothing he could do. Njal had told him to sit it out and threatened the chains if he disobeyed.

The darkness continued to envelop the area. Only the benches and the woman sat there. The white space had disappeared, and she rolled her eyes, looking annoyed. "Vitskertr."

No matter the training to control his anger. It was all he had. All that had happened in the last day caused him to doubt himself. The path he had wanted after the Warrior's Gate was to uncover his past, and now this woman knew and would not share the details with him.

"Who are you?!" Tyr yelled as the darkness closed in.

"Hel…Hele…" Her voice was drowned out as darkness enveloped them both.

Tyr woke up startled. He looked around and started to sit up. Then he felt a cool hand touch his chest and push him back down. "Lie down. Everything is okay."

It was Revna.

He was covered in a cold sweat. His head was in her lap, and she leaned back against a pile of light furs. "Bad dream."

"What did you mean when you said 'Hel'?" she asked.

Tyr realized he had been talking in his sleep. He pushed himself up into a seated position and flung his legs off the side of his cot. His hand was covered in bloody bandages, but he could feel the relic still in his hand. "You heard that?"

"It woke me up. You started stirring, then yelled 'Hel.'"

Tyr started to open his mouth, then stopped. Usually he would have told anyone anything, but after the day he'd had…"Was just thinking of the place Gorm and his friends could go after all they did."

"Oh."

It hurt that he couldn't tell Revna the truth. He wanted to talk to her about the woman in his dreams, how she was connected to his past and had saved his life. But it wasn't the time. "We need to tell Njal we found the relic and rescue the hostages."

"Tyr. They left." Revna looked at him, and Tyr could feel the anger rising.

"Why would they leave? They don't have the relic. We need to stop them before they get any further." He pushed off the cot and started moving about the room to gather his things.

"Stop. We need to talk first." Revna stood up and grabbed him by the shoulders. "Stop!"

Tyr felt her hands forcing him to stop rummaging about the room.

"After you passed out, I couldn't remove the relic. It has become a part of you." She lifted his left hand. "I wrapped the puncture wounds in bandages and put a salve on them. Early this morning Njal came in to check on you and found us both."

"Did you tell him anything or show him the relic?"

"No."

"Why not!" Tyr pulled his hand away. "Without this, they are going…going to kill them."

"I know." She turned and paced the floor, then turned back. "I told Njal that you were angry and had hurt your hand in the process. That's when I offered to stay back and watch over you while they went after the hostages. I was going to tell him, but when he told me they found Erik and that they were taking him with them, I hesitated."

"Erik! He is a spion. Why would they take him with them?"

"Don't you think I asked that? They said it was better to have him with them instead of leaving him behind to cause more trouble."

Tyr lifted his hand to speak, then thought better of it. Revna had done the right thing. If they had taken the relic along with Erik, it would have put them at risk. She had only tried to protect him, and she was willing to stay behind when Liv was as much of a mor to her as she was to him.

"Now that we have the relic, we need to go after

them," Tyr said.

"That's the plan." She smiled at him. Her blue eyes sparkled in the morning light.

He looked at her for a moment, then turned and closed his mouth, wiping the drool off his face. "I'm tired," he said, recovering.

She laughed at him. "You know Njal isn't going to be happy that I lied to him. I told him that I was going to make sure you didn't do anything reckless like follow them, and that was my plan all along."

"Let's head out before anyone tries to stop us. We need to reach them before they get to Eski. We can make more of a plan on the road. Let's gather our things and head out."

"I'm in! There is a lot I want to ask you, especially about your encounter with the Voktere." Revna slapped Tyr on the shoulder as she passed him. "I'll save it for the road. Let's go."

# Chapter 7: Tethering Leske

Tyr and Revna gathered their belongings and took two horses from the stables but were caught by Sif. She understood their desire to go but was hesitant at first. Over Revna's objections, Tyr unwrapped his hand and showed Sif the relic. Sif relented, letting them take the horses and even providing additional provisions for the road.

Tyr caught Revna up on what had occurred during his meeting with the Voktere and Gorm. She found it interesting that they were so interested in Gorm. There had to be some connection between Njal and him.

They talked more in detail about how Knud had told Tyr to stop using the name in front of everyone. Interesting. Revna asked more in-depth questions about the spirit beasts he had encountered.

He recollected how the giant serpent had appeared, then the wolf. They'd caught him off guard. He remembered being confused at seeing them appear in such an ethereal form, translucent but natural, tangible creatures.

His run-in with Gorm had changed everything. They weren't just fighting the battle with warriors whose weapons could slice, maim, wound, and kill, though the warriors alone were tough enough.

He started to doubt himself. He was so confident he had become one of the best Kriger known. Then he'd barely beat Njal and lost a fight with a creature he had only heard about in stories, a creature whose eyes were still emblazoned in his mind. Eyes that showed the storm that resided within.

They journeyed for hours until dusk, when the sun started to set in the west. They had journeyed northwest and were still a couple of days' journey out. They found a small spring on their way up the mountain toward Eski and stopped. Snow had begun to fill the tracks of Njal and the others.

"How far behind them are we?" Tyr asked while he started the fire.

"Hours would be my guess." Revna tossed a pile of wood nearby and threw one log into the fire. "We'll catch them in the next day or so if we wake up early."

"Can't believe it." Tyr sat upon the leather he had laid out, leaning against the horse's saddle and pack they'd brought with them.

"What?"

"That two nights ago we were celebrating the Warrior's Gate. We had just become Krigere, and here we are at war with the Voktere again." Tyr picked at the snow around him.

"Feels like forever to me, though it was just the other

night. Haven't had much time to sleep and try to sort it out." She lay against a pack as well and rolled out leather skins on the snow. "The question I keep asking myself is why didn't they prepare us for the Voktere?" She took a bite of her jerky.

Tyr wondered the same. The history they had learned was from nearly two decades prior, the war with the Voktere. It spoke of ethereal creatures that had come under the control of the Voktere. Once, they and the Krigere had worked in harmony to build great fortifications. Then the Voktere had started to use their gifts for evil. They began to slay for sport and control the beasts in the village, then vied for power.

The history had been in Njal's time, and the stories he told had made every Vokter look evil. His parents and siblings were killed during the war between the two groups, and after eliminating the Vokter threat, the Krigere had abandoned Eski to start a new life.

Now they were at war once more. The Voktere hadn't been eliminated; in nearly two decades, they had grown stronger.

"Why didn't we prepare better? If Njal knew what they were capable of, then why didn't he prepare us better?" Tyr asked as he took a bite of jerky.

"Stubbornness. He thought that he had killed the last of them, and his pride blinded him to the truth. Now his people are being held hostage, our village is in chaos, and loved ones are gone." She glowered and tossed another log into the fire. "That blood is on Njal's hands."

"They wanted this. The hostages are just the collateral." Tyr unwrapped his hand. "Not even sure why it is so important."

"Then we are walking into a trap," Revna said bluntly.

"How so?"

"Think about how they positioned it. Hostages? They could have slaughtered the entire village and taken the relic themselves."

"I doubt it. I took three of them before they called those creatures. I was thrown off when they appeared from nowhere." Tyr slammed his hand into the snow. "I let my guard down."

"Don't beat yourself up. Seeing them for the first time would throw anyone off. From what you were telling me, and how quickly it happened, anyone's guard would drop." She tossed some snow at Tyr. "Seriously, let it go."

He smiled as the snow hit him. "I'll try."

"I need sleep. Feels like it's been a week already." Revna stretched out and lay down. Before setting her head down, she asked, "Take the first watch?"

"Yeah." Tyr reached over and took his shield and axe.

"Get some sleep. We got a long journey ahead of us."

Tyr stood up, checked on the horses, and found a strategic place to watch for the night. He returned to the fire from time to time to regain feeling in his limbs and hands, tossing a log into the fire to keep it burning.

The snow clouds started to clear, and he could see the stars shine brightly. The moon was a quarter full as it gave its diminishing light.

He thought of Liv and the others trapped with the Voktere. How were they faring through all of this? He wondered who Hele was and how she fit into all of this. He had never encountered her before last night. All of these years, she'd known about his past, and then, as he finally started to feel he was getting answers, he was pulled in another direction entirely.

Thoughts were going to be his downfall. He could feel his thoughts overwhelming and bringing him down in despair. The fight with Gorm had left him bruised physically and mentally. His ribs were slightly tender from the kick he had received, and his neck constantly itched from where the quill had pierced his skin.

Hele, or whoever she was, had said she'd saved him from death. Whatever she did had made the wounds much easier to deal with, as they had started to scab over more quickly than in their original course.

Looking back, he was proud of who he had become

when he completed the Warrior's Gate and found Liv and his friends there. It was at that moment he had gained acceptance. Being an orphan had made it difficult growing up. His adopted mor, Liv, had taken him in, but when she told him of his past and how she'd found him, he had longed for answers.

Impressing Njal and those who had taught him over the years was what he'd craved. Acceptance as one of their own. He'd worked his way up through the years, studying the fighting techniques and their history, though reading was challenging, since slowing his mind down to read was excruciating.

He persisted throughout the many years, earning his peers' respect. Becoming close to Revna and Erik had made it better. They'd stuck together through everything, helped each other master the techniques taught in class. He and Revna had even studied history together on many nights prior. She had a knack for it, and she knew the Vokter history best.

Erik had always been there for him when Liv was distracted and was needed elsewhere. Tyr had dined with Erik's family.

Years of trust were wasted now that his friend—nearly his brother—had handed him over to be killed. He wondered what had caused Erik to fall so far. How had Tyr not seen it before that day? His behavior was typical heading into battle. Erik was nervous, even before the Warrior's Gate. Then to be called a spion, not only an enemy but a Vokter. What had Erik gotten himself into that he could never confide in his friends? It left him without answers.

While the sounds of wild animals came and went through the night, nothing disturbed their camp. Revna woke to take watch hours later, and he found himself falling asleep before his head hit the ground.

"Fornyelse." His body felt the warm, melodious voice once more. "Fornyelse."

Tyr found himself in darkness as the voice whispered the words. Then light started to appear and reveal the sanctuary once more.

The lady sat upon the bench, her hands weaving to and fro as the words escaped her lips. "Fornyelse." She pronounced the last syllable and clasped her hands together. "Welcome, Tyr. It seems we have calmed your mind enough for you to speak with me."

Tyr approached and sat on the bench beside her.

"I didn't catch your name—you know…when I lost it." He waved toward the darkness and back toward the light surrounding the sanctuary.

"Helena, child." She had such a soft voice; it seemed to cut the wind with kindness as it reached his ears.

"Helena," he said, confirming. "Can you answer my questions now?"

"I cannot, child. Please, remain patient and calm. We'll discuss your questions as we progress through your leskes."

"Leskes?"

"Your tongue, it calls them…" She closed her eyes for a moment. "Lessons. Before we begin, there are a few things I wish to discuss with you. Do you have any questions first? Ones I can answer?" She gave a wink and nod of her head. He could see the bark upon her skin in detail. A leaf fell from her lovely green hair to the ground below, then another grew on her head to replace it.

"I want details about my past. Why they want this relic, where you came from…"

"Ah, I can touch briefly on the last one before we begin, though I warn you to control your emotions. The information I am about to share may cause impatience and leave you with more unanswered questions. Can you remain a calm child?"

Tyr wanted more information. His anxiety was peaking already, and he started to take deep breaths. "Give me a moment."

The anxiety had started to cause the darkness to thicken and make its way toward the sanctuary.

"Fornyelse." She waved her hands, and he felt it help alleviate the feeling. "Shall we begin?"

"Yes." He was awestruck at how she had done that. "You'll need to tell me how you did that…when you can."

"In time." She wove her hands and spoke the words once more, alleviating even more anxiousness. "Your question is to know where I came from? To answer that, I need to begin at what you are."

"What I am?" he interrupted.

"Impatient. Do not interrupt me." She waited for him to allow her to continue and acknowledge her. "You are a Vokter. The guardian of spirits. One who can tether themselves to spirits that have crossed over into the realm of the dead. The spirits must accept you as their guardian, though the Voktere have twisted spirits to bind them to their will and lose their own throughout the years. These Voktere are a plague and have destroyed the harmony between the spirits and their guardian.

"You have been trusted to be such a guardian, to tether yourself to these spirits and allow them to retain their own will while they assist you."

She paused for a moment before Tyr said anything. "I am a Vokter?" Even as he said the words, they struck him as false.

"Yes, child. Wait a moment while that sinks in."

He felt it sinking in. How had he never come to realize that he was a Vokter? That he had the ability to be the guardian of spirits? "How come I have never connected with the spirits if I am a Vokter, like you say? Shouldn't I have realized that already?"

"Calm," she said as the darkness started to push its way farther inward. "It brings us to the first leske."

Tyr glanced around and then started to breathe deeply, slowing the darkness as it continued forward. "Trying. It's a lot to take in."

"Fornyelse." She waved her hands, and he felt it help alleviate the anxiety. "I won't be able to continue renewing your mind like this." Leaves fell from her hair, and they didn't reappear this time.

"Please, continue."

"Good. Now let us begin your first leske." She stood and sat beside him. "I'm about to teach you how to tether yourself to a spirit. Once the host has been slain or killed, a part of the host's body must be retained. An example would be a hawk." She waved her hand, and a hawk glided through the air and landed upon the bench. "Once the hawk is slain, you'll take feathers or skin from its body and craft a totem to be worn upon yourself or a place near you. Once the article has been made, call to the host's spirit while holding the totem before you. The call isn't audible but more inward. Feel yourself connecting outside of yourself.

"Once the spirit has appeared, it will communicate within your mind's eye. Once it's accepted you as its guardian, the tethering shall begin. It is the form of weaving the spirit and body together into the article you have made."

She stepped forward and approached the hawk, which lay down and died. She flicked her fingernails, and Tyr saw them become sharp. She carved the skin of the hawk, yanked out a few feathers, and came beside Tyr once more.

She wove the feathers into the leather of a small bracelet, then called the hawk. It appeared before her in a spiritual form, and it sat perched on the ground before her.

She then held the article in one hand and began weaving an invisible thread through the bracelet. She wove runes within the leather, and the hawk bowed its head and disappeared.

"I have given the hawk a name. By weaving the runes into the leather, I have now become its guardian." She held up the bracelet.

"What runes did you weave?" Tyr asked.

"They spell the name I have given the spirit." She held the bracelet out to him.

He took it and inspected the runes. "Sky," he said.

"Yes." She waved her hands, and the body and leather bracelet disappeared. "Remember the leske you were taught today. We are guardians of these spirits, not enforcers. Tethering works with the host spirit to become its guardian. This concludes our first lesson." She waved her hands, and the light around the sanctuary started to diminish.

"Wait. I have questions," Tyr called as she turned toward him.

"Impatient child, I am tired." She waved her hand again, and a handful of leaves fell around her as darkness filled the space.

Tyr shot up out of the snow. "Wait."

Revna came to his side. "Wait for what?"

Tyr glanced around as the sun started to lift from the east, the light breaking over the mountain ridge. It had all been a dream. "I asked someone to wait in my dream."

"Who?"

He thought about it for a moment; he could trust Revna. She hadn't betrayed him as Erik had after all these years. It wasn't fair that he had started to keep things from her just because of what Erik had done to him the other day.

Tyr didn't know how she would take the fact that he was a Vokter. Maybe she wouldn't want anything to do with him. It was tied to his past, which meant it had everything to do with his goals to learn more about it. He took his chances. "Helena."

He then told her about the dreams he had just had.

# Chapter 8: The Voktere

"You're a Vokter?" Revna sat awestruck after Tyr had finished telling her the dreams.

"Yes, that is what Helena said," Tyr responded.

"The girl that looks like a moving tree—she told you that you were a Vokter? Unbelievable. How come you didn't show any signs before the other day?"

Tyr had asked himself the same question. "Helena is limited in what she can and cannot tell me. I'll get that answer soon enough if I keep having the same dreams. Happened two nights in a row, so it should happen again tonight."

"Can't believe it. This whole time you've been a Vokter. This changes everything." She stood up in excitement.

"Changes what?"

"Everything we learned from the history books. They said that every Vokter was evil, but I look at you and know the books can't be true."

Tyr gave a sigh of relief. The worry washed away, hearing her talk like this. After he had told her that he was a Vokter, he thought she would panic and run away. It had all seemed strange to him, but having someone to share that knowledge with made it an easier burden to carry.

"Call something, anything." She knelt in the snow, waiting.

"I can't. Helena said I needed to tether to the spirit. I haven't done any of that." He looked up at her, his hands in the air empty before him. "I just learned I was a Vokter."

"Right, right. Tethering. You need to become its guardian. What was the other word she used to describe those who don't become guardians but force their own wills on the spirits?"

"Enforcers."

"Right, right. Hold up, I just got an idea. Follow me." She grabbed his hand and pulled him up from his leather mat. "Get your bow."

"Where are we going?" he said as she pulled him away from camp.

"To find breakfast. I'm starving. And you're going to do that whole tethering thing."

He found himself tripping over his feet as she pulled him along through the snow and out toward the horses, where he grabbed his bow as they rushed past.

The branches hung low, covered with heavy snow. The mountain shone with majesty, covered with snow and jutting rock faces. The sun was bright in the sky, but the cold winds that had settled in the valley kept the snow from melting. Clouds fought their way through the sky, bringing fresh wind and snow in their wake.

Tyr and Revna crept forward through the snow, scouting for life. They had come across a family of elk but had scared them off in their hurry to hunt breakfast.

Revna had her bow drawn and arrow nocked, ready to fire.

They kept their talking to a minimum and crept along, lightening their steps to keep from crunching the snow.

A deer bounded through the open snow about twenty yards off. Revna waved Tyr forward.

The deer lifted its head as he moved but then went back to digging through the snow to find fresh grass.

Tyr watched as Revna pulled the bowstring back, aimed, and released.

The deer, spooked by another sound, bounded away. The arrow sank into the snow where the deer had just been. A handful of white rabbits hopped through the snow a couple of yards away. They hadn't been easy to spot in the snow.

Tyr drew his bowstring back and let the arrow soar. It struck one of the rabbits. Revna had nocked and released an arrow of her own, hitting another rabbit.

The other rabbits hopped away quickly through the snow, leaving their friends and paw prints behind them.

They walked over to the downed rabbits and lifted them out of the snow.

"Guess we're having rabbit for breakfast." Tyr lifted a sizeable white rabbit by the ears.

Revna lifted hers as well. "Jerky for the road." She smiled.

Revna skinned and dressed the rabbit, rubbed some honey over its flesh, and ran a spit through its body. Then she turned it slowly over the fire.

Tyr stretched his rabbit out to full length. Finding the longest foot, he cut it off close to the joint. He placed the rabbit to the side, then brought out a copper bowl from his pack. He loaded snow into the bowl and held it over the fire. Then he washed and prepared the rabbit foot, rinsing the blood away and draining it. He placed the foot near the fire to dry.

He lifted the rabbit's body, skinned it, and dressed it. A large piece of fur he washed and placed near the fire to dry. He proceeded to slice thin pieces of meat and put them into another small bowl from the pack.

Revna watched him as she roasted her rabbit, and he caught her glance a few times as he worked away at preparing the jerky for the road.

"We'll see how this all goes. To be honest, I don't feel

like a Vokter, or even know what they feel like," Tyr said as he sliced strips of meat and placed them in the bowl.

"According to the history books, at least if you look deeply enough, only a handful of the Krigere had started to feel a connection to the beasts that they had slain. The history began to be erased after that. They had found a way to connect with the animals and then call them, but the books didn't go into any detail on how. I bet Njal made sure that nothing anyone would ever read would describe how they did it, in case he hadn't eliminated every last one of the Voktere." She continued to inspect the rabbit and then continued to roast it on the uncooked sides.

"Without knowing what Helena said, I don't think I would even know where to start." He reached over and lifted the rabbit's foot. "After breakfast, I'll attempt tethering the spirit to this rabbit's foot." He placed it back down near the fire to dry.

"I should have cut this rabbit's foot off before I roasted it. Then I could have tried tethering to it." She continued to turn the spit. "I'll watch how you do it. Then maybe I'll give it a go the next time we need food."

"I wonder what Njal would think if not only I showed up as a Vokter, but you did too."

"He'd lose his mind." She paused. "I don't think he would like it at all. Best to keep it to ourselves. I'm still trying to piece it all together myself."

Tyr finished slicing the meat and washed his hands in the snow. Revna finished cooking the rabbit and cut pieces off for them to eat. They placed the strips of meat Tyr had sliced into the fire as they sat together eating breakfast.


The white rabbit's foot sat in Tyr's hands. He had made a small hole and placed a leather loop through it.

He glanced down and didn't know how to make himself begin. He felt like seconds had gone by while he held the foot, only to realize it had been minutes because Revna told him to not waste any more daylight.

He lifted the foot with his left hand and closed his eyes. Nothing happened. He opened his eyes. "Nothing is happening."

"Just relax. You're too focused on your physical self. Focus on what is inside you. Find that spirit within yourself. Discard your physical side for a moment, your desires, needs, and wants. Focus on how you became bound to your own body through your spirit." Revna looked impatiently at him, but she was calm in her message.

Tyr closed his eyes. His thoughts immediately went over the material things he had wanted in life. Strength, security, and family. Tangible items that he could touch, strength from training his body, and safety in his surroundings.

He thought about how his eyes had shown him the beautiful world around him. The beautiful things the world had to offer. His eyes. They allowed his spirit to see his surroundings, to pass images from a physical realm of tangible things into his mind.

His spirit had been chosen to live this life within this body and none other. A body that carried the traits of his parents and their parents before. But his spirit was unique. Everyone might receive looks and characteristics of their parents, but each came into the world with their personality.

He thought of his mor, the one he had never known. Could he bring her image before him from the depths of his mind? Could he connect to her? Where was she now? Had she passed over into the realm of spirits, or was she still out there?

Fire lit in his heart. A burning. He lifted his left hand again and felt a watchful eye and movement in the space around him.

He opened his eyes and saw a rabbit sitting on its hind legs behind him in the snow. A translucent glow surrounded its body in its ethereal form.

"*I have come.*" He heard the voice within his mind.

"*You can speak?*" Tyr asked within his mind as he spoke to the rabbit.

The rabbit nodded.

In his heart, he knew that this animal had given its life to provide food and nourishment to him and Revna. "*Thank you for giving your life to provide for our needs.*" He knew he had to say it; the burning was there. This rabbit had given its physical form to provide for his. "*We are honored.*"

"*You have called to me. What do you wish of me?*" it said within his mind.

"*I desire to become your guardian, to bind your soul back to the physical realm that you might aid me.*"

The rabbit sat for a moment and then nodded. No voices passed then, but the rabbit gave its acceptance to become tethered.

"*Kanin.*" Tyr knew the rabbit's name as it accepted his offer. With his right hand, he then started to weave the invisible thread into the rabbit's foot until he had inscribed the name Kanin into it.

Kanin, the rabbit, looked up once more and then nodded as it dissipated into the air. Then Tyr felt the air around him change, and the noise of the wind hit his ears.

"Tyr, can you hear me?" Revna was snapping her fingers. "You were in a trance, and you started moving your hands around the rabbit's foot. It was kind of scary."

"Did you see it?"

"See what?"

"The rabbit was right there." Tyr pointed at the snow. There were no paw prints or anything to show that a rabbit had been there. "I swear it was right there, and we talked to each other. Or at least communicated within my mind." He shook his head. "Made sense at the time, but looking back, it sounds odd."

"I didn't see anything. Though I could see runes appear and disappear on the rabbit's foot as you moved your hands about it. What runes were they?" She reached out to the rabbit's foot. "Can I see it?"

He handed her the rabbit's foot. "The name Kanin."

She rubbed the foot. "Can barely see them." She handed it back to him.

"Can't believe it. I'm a Vokter." Then the realization hit him that all his life, he had grown up hating the Voktere, only to find out that he was now one of them. "Njal is going to kill me."

"Can you call it?" Revna asked impatiently. "After all the history and reading about them, I want to know more."

"Let me try." Tyr tied the rabbit's foot to his leggings and secured it.

The moment he started to close his eyes to figure out how to reach out to Kanin, hooves pounded into the snow, and he saw two men riding toward their camp at full speed.

"Gorm sends his regards!" one of the men yelled as they closed the gap.

# Chapter 9: Caught a Foot

The rushing hooves crunched through the snow, edging toward the camp. Tyr rushed toward his pack as one of the horses flew through their camp. It ran through the fire, and he saw the glint of steel aimed directly at him.

He leaped to the side, avoiding the sword, but fell face-first into the snow. He pushed himself up and scrambled forward to his pack. The horse had started around. Revna was engaged with the other rider, a skinning knife in her hands; at least she was on her feet, Tyr thought as he lifted his axe and shield and found the horse running right at him.

He started to roll to his left onto his shield when he felt steel slice into his shoulder. His roll brought the blade off his shoulder and down his backside.

Rolling to his feet, he felt the warm sensation of blood on his back. He breathed, allowing it to flow into a controlled rage. The horse was making its new round, and Tyr rushed toward the rider.

The horse headed toward him once more, and he looked for the opening on the horse's right side. He made his way to the right of the horse, sending his shield into the horse's head and rolling out of the way. The sword dipped for him again, and the horse swerved and neighed. The rider slowed the horse and slid off the side.

Tyr finally took a moment to look at whom he'd been fighting. His head was bald, the skin tight, while his beard was braided into two long strands. He carried a large sword and wore leather armor that left his chest bare, with a strap across the front to hold the shoulder and side pieces together. His right arm was covered with leather skins from shoulder to wrist in a scaly fashion, while his left arm was layered with a thick covering made of a material Tyr had rarely seen.

Troll skin.

"Gorm told me you'd be hard to kill," the man said, a smile on his face. "I was willing to take the bet, but the money isn't worth anything if I'm dead."

"I'm going down the list until I get to Gorm myself," Tyr replied, moving his shield into the defensive position, axe at his side.

Runes flared on the man's left arm, and the troll hide lit up for a moment. Then a troll appeared beside the man, stretching its back. It was seven feet tall, with a broad chest and wretched face, its eyes large, its mouth flanked by tusks, its arms long and lanky. The ethereal gray skin was tight, stretched to the limit. The muscles pushed against the skin as if wanting to escape their confinement. The belly was bloated, and Tyr could now recognize the spiritual glow surrounding it.

Tyr looked up and glanced back between the two. He had faced smaller trolls during hunting raids near the mountains, but none this size.

He caught Revna at the side fighting against the other…Vokter. She was being attacked by a wolf and bear as well as the Vokter.

"The list stops here." The man lifted his finger, and the troll roared forward, its giant fist heading toward Tyr's head.

Tyr lifted his shield to block the fist, and it drove him to his knee. With one knee planted on the ground, he braced himself as the pounding continued. He swung his axe at the troll.

His arm was knocked to the side, and the axe slipped out of his grasp. His shield rocked again, and the troll swung at his side.

He fell back into the snow, and the fist skipped off the top of the shield. The troll stepped forward, the swordsman right behind, placed both hands together, and brought them downward.

Tyr lifted his shield, and the wind was knocked cold out of him. He gasped for air as the troll lifted its hands and repeated the blow. His shield was there to block the impact, and again his world danced with stars. The wood creaked under the strain, and his hand fell to the side. The troll started to raise its hands into the air.

"*Fornyelse.*" Tyr heard the voice, and he was filled with new breath, renewed strength.

He rolled to the side and onto his knee just in time. The troll's fists hit the ground where he had been seconds before.

"*Kanin, harness, do not call.*" The voice echoed in his mind.

He glanced down and saw the rabbit's foot and started to call to Kanin. "*Harness.*" He stopped and reached toward Kanin to make use of the rabbit he had tethered to.

The world slowed around him. He felt light on his feet, and he could better observe things as they were happening around him. The troll's hands were sweeping toward him. He ducked gracefully and looked for his axe, then rushed toward it. He felt like he should zigzag along the way but kept his course straight. He lifted the axe and turned, feeling renewed once more, shield raised before him.

He felt his wits about him. Keen mental sharpness, quickness. He knew what to do.

The snow dusted behind him as his feet flew off the ground. The troll's eyes went wide as it swung its fist and found the air where Tyr had been. Tyr's axe buried itself into the side of the troll, and Tyr bounded past.

The troll's roar brought snow falling from trees

around them. Its roar settled into a growl, and its teeth ground together. Tyr had turned and waited for the troll to turn as he brought the axe upward into the neck. The troll gurgled and disappeared into the air; mist followed.

Tyr felt blunt force against his back and fell forward, arms wide. He hit the snow and rolled to his right side, and he saw the sword as he turned. Tyr moved his shoulder in its path and felt the pressure in his left arm. The wood prevented the blade from reaching his skin, but the pressure was there.

Tyr still felt his keen wits about him, and he kicked the warrior's foot and connected. He tumbled backward into the snow. Tyr was off the ground and rushed forward to slam his shield into the man's chest and felt the world speed up once more. He tripped over his feet and went headlong over the man. His quickness, wits, and observation were gone.

He slammed into his shield arm with his chest and hit the snow. He sucked in his breath, trying to recover as he turned to find the warrior on his feet. The sword plunged downward toward his guts.

The snapping of a bowstring brought an arrow through the man's neck. He stumbled, and the sword slid into the snow beside Tyr. The body fell on top of him.

Tyr pushed to move the man off of him and tried to

catch his breath, but it was too much.

He felt the body pulled off of him and found Revna staring down at him. "What would you do without me?" She reached out a hand and pulled him up.

Tyr stood and caught his breath for a moment and found the other warrior in the snow. His eyelids were scratched up badly, and his eyes had dark holes. "How did that happen?"

She lifted her hunting knife from her side. "Had to use what I had, though I didn't get away without a few scrapes of my own."

Deep claw marks were across her leather armor, the stomach area ripped open, and small slices of blood could be seen. Her arms had teeth marks, and blood flecked her face. "Bear caught me by surprise, and the wolf got a good hold on my arm. Was able to break away and went right for the warrior—or Vokter, I knew, when I realized he had called them."

She cleaned the firepit of the scattered wood and started a new fire to heat bowls of water. She pulled healing salves out and applied them to her clean wounds, then cleaned and dressed Tyr's wounds.

"Hadn't expected we'd run into them out here, and so early in the morning." Tyr rubbed his chest where the troll had pounded his shield into it repeatedly. "Feels like he broke a rib. Hurts when I breathe."

"It's going to be sore for a while. Take off your chest piece and let me wrap it." She reached over to help unclasp his leather armor and started to wrap his chest and ribs.

"Ow! That hurts."

"Stop being such a child and hold still." She continued to wrap, and Tyr let a few more *ow*s out as she did so.

"Fighting the Voktere changes everything we learned growing up." Tyr lay back, the white wrapping around his chest. "Fighting warriors is one thing, but did you see the size of that troll?"

"Njal should have prepared the Krigere for it." Revna had venom in her voice. "His arrogance cost people their lives, and believing that he had truly rid the world of Voktere? Unwise."

Tyr had only heard Revna speak with such venom a few times prior. Once was when she had just lost her mor, and another was during an argument with Njal and Sif about her far. Her mor's dying wish was for them to tell Revna more about her far and what had happened to him, but they'd kept it from her. Eventually she let it go, but Tyr knew that it had always been a sore spot for her, as his past had been for him.

"Now you're one of them…" She caught herself. "Your heart is different than the ones we faced today. I didn't mean it to come out that way."

"It's okay." Tyr felt the sting. He knew that if Njal or the others found out, he would be a footnote in the history books, a hiccup along the way to ridding the world of the Voktere. "Been only a couple of hours since I found out myself."

"I know. Everything is happening so fast, and it's just all in the forefront of my mind. All being jumbled together right now." She shook her head, her hands waving in front of her face. "A lot to take in."

Tyr let it lie at that. Looking back at the fight with the Voktere from moments ago, he thought about how he had heard Helena's voice. She had given him a renewed strength, and then he had harnessed Kanin. He lifted the rabbit's foot tied to his leather leggings and thought how his wits had never been so clear to him. He could see everything as it was happening before his eyes. The way he had planned it all so fast and brought the troll down. Then it all left as quickly as it had come.

It was something he would bring up with Helena when he could speak with her again. He wanted to share the details with Revna but knew she was going through a lot at the moment.

She was throwing things into her pack, anger evident in her movements. Tyr sat on his pack and looked toward the sky as the sun started to progress toward noonday.

Would the Krigere accept him once they had found out that one of their own was a Vokter, but he wasn't one of them? He had been adopted into the tribe by Liv as a child. His parents were unknown. Helena was strange and new in his life, unable to share the secrets of his past at this moment.

Pieces had started to fall into place in his mind. Not being raised as one of the Kriger children made sense now. Njal had spent years neglecting him or not wanting to allow him to participate with the other children. Persistence ran its course, though, and Tyr had been accepted. He had built the strength on his own, made friends around him, and never given in and quit or left on his own. The security of the village had become his home, his family, and he had a mor, Liv.

Her love and determination broke down the barriers surrounding Njal's heart and helped Tyr be accepted by them. That was why she was so proud of him when he completed the Warriors Gate. But now she was gone. Taken by one of the most hated people around, a Vokter. Njal was going after them with the Krigere, and Tyr had a feeling if Njal found out that he was a Vokter now, it wouldn't go over well, regardless of his being accepted or not.

"Pack your stuff and let's get moving." Revna stood behind him, her face cutting into his view, then kicked his pack. "I'm not doing it for you."

"Okay." He started to move, and she kicked the pack again. His ribs burned. "Ow, okay."


Tyr finished packing his belongings and saddled the horse, his pack thrown over it. They had set the warriors' horses free and taken the belongings from the dead. Tyr glanced back at the carnage of the battle fought here, at the scattered firewood, the two dead bodies in the snow and tracks everywhere, then mounted his horse. The aches and pains were very evident as he did so.

"*Fornyelse.*" The voice echoed in his mind, and his pain eased. "*Tyr, we need to speak.*"

"*How?*" Tyr asked in his mind.

"*Fornyelse…I've given you enough strength to speak with me for a moment. Please remain calm.*"

Helena then appeared beside his horse, the mystical glow surrounding her. She placed a bark-skinned hand on the horse's head and grabbed the reins. Her green hair danced in the rushing wind, and leaves danced in her hair and shifted ever so slightly. Then she smiled, and her light-green eyes sparkled. She was lean and tall and beautiful to behold. Green ivy danced down her body, covering her in a flowing dress.

"*There isn't much time, and only you can hear or see me.*" She spoke within his mind once more. "*These spirits cannot remain tethered without a guardian.*" She waved at the bodies that lay in the snow. "*Take the totems upon the bodies, and speak with the spirit, unbinding them from the mortal realm…*" Leaves started to fall around her, and her body began to flicker.

"*You want me to unbind—*"

"*Child! Untether their spirits from this realm. Voktere must be guardians, not enforcers. Unless you unbind these spirits or give them free will, they will come for you.*" She flickered again as a handful of leaves fell from her hair.

"*Who will come?*" Tyr asked in his mind.

"What are you doing or looking at? Let's go, Tyr." Revna had moved beside him. Tyr waved a hand at her.

"*The Fenrixes, child.*" Helena smiled at him, and the last leaf fell from her hair. "*The Fenrixes.*" Then a burst of wind shattered the air.

The horses spooked, and the wind pushed their manes back. Tyr looked at Revna.

"What was that?" she asked.

"Helena, we need to untether the spirits from the Vokter we killed." Tyr kicked his horse forward.

Revna kicked her horse too, and it sped around him when he stopped and jumped down to the ground. She glared down at him. "We need to go. They need the relic, or they're going to start killing the hostages." Her voice softened a pitch. "Liv."

Tyr stopped in his tracks, realizing that without the relic, he would be sentencing his mor to death. "You're right." He didn't want anything to happen to Liv or the others taken by the Voktere. However, Helena was connected to his past. The past that had remained hidden from him his entire life. He had to do this if he wanted to get the answers he was after. He looked up at Revna. "I have to do this," he told her and turned to walk over to the body of the Vokter.

# Chapter 10: The Hunted Wolf

Tyr started to pull the totems off the Vokter upon the ground. Revna relented and came to help him find the totems. They had to peel the leather off the Vokter's arm. Then they looked for anything that might resemble a totem.

They made a pile of the totems and tossed the last one in. There was a troll hide, a clawed bear shoulder pad, a wolf pelt made into a small cloak, and a serpent's skin that had wrapped the man's arm.

Tyr wondered why the man hadn't called to the serpent—another unanswered question in his mind. He stared down at the totems and didn't know where to begin. He had just learned how to tether a spirit to a totem, and now he was to untether a spirit he hadn't bound to this realm.

"Going to start with this one." He lifted the serpent's skin and instantly felt a surge of shock rush through his body. He dropped it. "Never mind, too many memories there. I may just do the troll first, since I had just interacted with it."

He moved the troll hide to the side and knelt next to it. *It should just be like tethering*, he thought as he held the leather.

Nothing.

He tried again, trying to clear his mind, taking deep breaths in and out. Then he called to the troll.

The wind picked up behind him, and he felt the cold breeze off the mountainside rush past him. Then nothing.

"That's not working." Tyr dropped the hide into the snow and stood up. "Thought it would work just like it had when I tethered to the rabbit, but nothing."

"Can't we just bring them with us and figure it out later?" Revna asked, standing beside him. "We're losing daylight, and we can't continue to waste it."

She was right, and Tyr knew it. Any time wasted was time they were running against. Helena had been sure that he should do it now and not wait. She hadn't said anything about not taking the totems with them, but she was urgent about it now.

"I need to try again, and if it doesn't work, we'll go." He reached down and lifted the troll hide.

"What do the runes say? Aren't you supposed to bind it with a name?" Revna looked over his shoulder, inspecting the hide. "Right there. It's light but visible."

Tyr looked at where she had pointed and found the runes. "T-R-O-L-L." He spelled out the letters. "Oh, very original."

Revna laughed. "How sweet."

Tyr lifted the troll's hide and called to it within his

mind. *Troll, come.*

The runes flared light blue. Then the troll appeared before Tyr. However, the soft glow surrounding his body had been replaced by a slight red hue. The troll was agitated and glared at Tyr and down at his hide. His fists were raised.

Tyr lifted his hand. "Stop. I am here to free you."

The troll hesitated and tilted its head to the side, confused. "Free?"

"Yes." Tyr reached down and started to pull at the invisible threads that bound the spirit to its hide. He began to unravel the runes woven into the hide. The troll stomped before him.

"Nei!" The troll turned in place, and the snow kicked up around him.

"Hurry," Revna said in a whisper.

"I'm trying." Tyr started to rush, and his hand slipped on the invisible thread.

"Nei! Nei!" The troll fell to its knees and grabbed its skull.

Tyr could make out a dark outline surrounding the red hue. He felt something was wrong, and in his panic he had started to rush. He took a deep breath and calmed his mind as Helena had been trying to tell him to do. Then started to untether the rest of the runes. He could see the pain and anguish this caused the troll, and he felt the pain and suffering. The troll had lost its own free will and had done the bidding of its enforcer.

Tyr's hands moved delicately on the runes. Each thread he pulled back eased the pain caused to the spirit before him. He could feel the strain removed from the troll and felt its mind returning to its own will.

The troll's hands slowly slid from its skull, and it glanced up at Tyr as the red hue dissipated. Its light blue eyes bore into Tyr and gave thanks for what he had just done, and he could see a tear roll down its face. Then, with a nod, it stood up and walked away and dissolved into the air.

The last thread snapped, and when the troll vanished, Tyr felt the air around him burst. His hair blew back as the wind expanded and collapsed inward with an audible pop.

Tyr sighed in relief. "I thought he was going to kill me."

"He was angry," Revna said beside him. She let out a sigh of her own. "How many more of these do we have?"

"Three…You saw that, then?" Tyr asked. He had thought only he could see the spirits when he touched the leather to bind them, but Revna had seen that one.

"Yeah, why?"

"Did you see the rabbit when I bound to it?" Tyr was

curious.

"No, didn't see that, but saw that red troll." She pointed to where the troll had been and then waved a hand in front of Tyr's face. "Hurry up. We've got to finish these up and get on the road."

Tyr pulled his axe and shield close to his body and laid the hide on the ground. He wasn't about to get wrapped up by another serpent. The serpent acted in the same manner as the troll but never attacked.

He unraveled the bear the same way, and the air around them collapsed with another audible pop.

"One left." He lifted the wolf hide, then called to the wolf by its name. *Wolf.* Tyr felt, as he had with the others, that the names were primary. Had he done it wrong by giving the rabbit an actual name? The thought passed through his mind as the wolf appeared, covered in the red hue.

The wolf's untethering went the same as the others', but right before the wolf turned to leave, it looked up at Tyr and placed its paw on the pelt in his lap.

"My mother hunted. Find her and bring me home. Follow the path northwest and find my home in the mountain." The wolf took off northwest, the direction Revna and Tyr needed to go, and disappeared.

Tyr glanced toward Revna and gave her an awkward smile. She knew something was up right away. It was the look he always gave when something was amiss.

"What now?" she asked, annoyed.

"Nothing, we can go now." He stood up and brought only the wolf pelt with him toward the horses.

"No, no, no. I can tell something is up. What did that wolf tell you?"

"Nothing. Let's go." He shoved the pelt into the pack and mounted the horse. She folded her arms and gave him a defiant glare. She wasn't going to budge until he told her. "The wolf just wanted me to bring him home." He pointed northwest. "We're heading in that direction anyway."

"Might as well just go home. We're not going to make it if we keep stopping." She kicked the snow and pulled herself onto her horse. "You and your soft heart. It's going to get a lot of people killed." She kicked her horse forward.

"Oh, don't be like that," he said, following her. "Just keep your eyes out for a cave in the mountain as we head that way."

He heard her release a drawn-out sigh and then sent her horse into a sprint. Tyr urged his horse to try and keep up.


They traveled for over an hour. The trees thinned as

they left their village farther behind and neared the mountains. They crossed more of the snowy open fields between the skog and the mountainside, which reflected the light off its crystalline surface. Their horses maintained an incredible speed in the open fields. The wildlife bounded to the sides as they passed.

Tyr had to suppress the urge to stop himself from going after every animal to create a new pelt. But the jerky they had made would last them for the next day or so, and slaughtering innocent animals just for the hunt wasn't in the cards for him.

After feeling the surge of harnessing Kanin from the totem, it left him wanting more. The way his mind had become when he harnessed Kanin—it made him twitch in anticipation of doing it again. He lifted the rabbit's foot with his right hand and glanced down at it, the runes for Kanin's name woven into it. The history books had never given this much information on how useful these totems could be. They'd only talked about the destruction that had occurred when the gift was used for evil purposes.

He refocused on the road and kept pace with Revna, who rarely spoke to him. He thought about how he was going to convince Njal that he wasn't like the Voktere in the history books. Could they work it out, or would Njal treat him as he had the ones in the books? It was an issue for Tyr to overcome, and the idea of losing

Njal's acceptance gave him anxiety.

He gritted his teeth, trying to push the thoughts aside as Liv came to his mind. How would she react? Would she still love him and be proud of the son she had raised, or would she abandon him? The anxiousness spiked, and he could feel his head pulsing and his heart racing.

"*Fornyelse.*" The voice came to his mind. "*Breathe. Harnessing your totems can cause you to feel connected to the animal and feel their anxiety too. Unharness yourself and breathe.*"

Tyr glanced down and saw the runes upon the totem. He took a deep breath and let his thoughts unharness him from Kanin. The runes shaded back to a light gray upon the rabbit's foot.

"Helena?" Tyr called out.

"*We'll speak soon, child. You are in constant need of renewal, and it wears me thin. I must rest now.*"

Tyr attempted to call her again and got nothing in reply. He had felt himself going paranoid after he took his eyes off the totem. He felt skittish, and his thoughts had raced from Njal to Liv, and his heart beat rapidly, as if fear was taking over his mind. He felt calmer now that he had unharnessed the totem and thought that he was in a better mindset.

Revna had slowed her pace and raised her hand to her ear. "Hear that?"

"Hear what?" Tyr slowed his horse to a trot beside her. He had been focused on other things.

"Listen."

He did. The wind. The crunching of hooves hitting the snow as they trotted together. The rustle of their packs. Then he heard it. Howling.

"It's coming from the west." Tyr kicked his horse into a sprint and headed closer to the mountains.

"Wait!" Revna called from behind him.

Tyr hoofed it up the hill, and the howling became louder. Trees covered his way as he approached the mountainside. Rocks had tumbled and crushed trees in their wake. He looked at which way to go and heard the howl coming across the destroyed trees and rocks. He pushed his horse forward and stepped slowly over the wreckage.

"Wait, you half-troll!" growled Revna from behind him.

"That howl is one of pain. We need to get there." He crossed the wreckage and rode hard up another small hill. The horse pushed hard through the snow as it slid under its hooves.

Tyr crested the hilltop and found an open area beside the mountainside. A large cave sat within the rock. The snow was trampled and covered with drops of blood around the opening.

There were very few trees in the area. Tyr spotted one man standing near a tree, crossbow being drawn back with another bolt. Another man covered in leather and furs stood in the cave entrance holding a flail. One man's body was tossed to the side. The crimson pool around it made Tyr guess they were already dead. Around the area were smaller wolves, their bodies mangled and lying still in the snow, blood splattered on their fur.

Then he spotted an enormous wolf outside the cave. Its bluish fur stood on end, and blood dripped from its sides where bolts protruded. The wolf's mouth was up in a snarl, with sharp canine teeth protruding past its lips.

The man rushed forward and threw the chain with unseen strength. The wolf brought its paw down upon the chain, grabbed it in its teeth, and yanked the man back. Then with blurred speed it snapped its jaw against the man's throat and tossed his lifeless body to the side.

Then the wolf howled as the crossbow snapped. The bolt struck right beside the wolf's neck, and it staggered sidelong into the snow, its paws giving way.

The man stepped forward, drawing another bolt and setting it. He started to pull it back as he spotted Tyr.

Tyr kicked his horse into motion, reaching back and lifting his shield. He then reached inward to harness

Kanin.

Stars flew before his eyes, sharp pain erupted in his skull, and he dropped his shield and fell off his horse.

He felt the cold snow hit his face and could only focus on the pain in his skull.

He heard the crunching of snow around him but couldn't move. "Foolish boy. Do you know how many wolves we had to kill to get their mor to come out? We lost a bunch of good men to catch this one. What's another body?"

Tyr heard the snapping of the string and felt no additional pain, just a loud grunt.

"Leave him alone." He heard Revna's voice—or was it her voice? It all was becoming muddled together.

He heard shuffling around him, and try as he might, he couldn't get past the spiked numbness in his mind. He pushed up to his elbows and sat there catching his breath and found Revna engaged in combat with the man and saw the spirit birds around her. She dodged and glided past the birds, striking at the man. He parried and caught her in the arm, and she stepped back.

Tyr pushed himself up more. "Revna." He watched as the bird positioned its head above her, then started to spiral. She pulled out her hunting knife with her other arm and tossed it. It struck the man, and he fell to his knees then face-first into the snow. The birds dissolved before reaching Revna's head, and she turned, rushing to Tyr's side.

"Are you all right?" she asked, looking around his body. "Where did he hit you?"

"I don't know. My head hurts bad." He lifted his hand to his head.

"There is nothing there. Are you sure?"

"I'm sure. Can't focus. It's subsiding little by little. I'll be fine. How is your arm?" He reached toward the blood on her right arm.

"He got lucky." She wiped at the blood. "Not a deep cut."

The wolf's howls fell into whimpers. It was struggling to crawl toward the dead wolves.

Tyr tapped his skull, trying to clear the pain. No use. "Get the pelt," he said, continuing to tap his head. *Come on, Helena!* he called inwardly.

"Are you joking? Look at that thing. I'm not going near it until it's dead." Revna threw an arm under his. "Let's get you to your feet."

He stood up, and the pain eased more. He took deep breaths. "I don't know what happened. One second I'm fine, the next I'm in the snow, enormous pain in my head." Then he remembered what he had been trying to do before it hit him. "I was trying to harness Kanin, and it knocked me flat."

He flung his hand against the rabbit's foot totem.

"Interesting," Revna said, but he felt she wanted to say more.

Tyr watched as the mother reached the wolves in the snow and picked them up in her mouth. She was on her feet, stumbling about to bring the bodies together near the entrance to the cave. He saw the wolf reach up with her paw, trying to pull at the bolt in its neck.

The pain had nearly all subsided, now a just dull thudding in his head. "I need to give the pelt back and remove that bolt," he said, walking toward his horse, picking his shield up along the way.

"You're going to get yourself killed!" Revna pulled at his shoulder. "We aren't here to do this, and you know it."

Tyr looked at her and back at the wolf. "She is dying. I want to keep the promise I made to her pup."

"You owe this beast nothing. The people who are being held hostage are the ones you should be thinking about." She reached down and touched the relic in his hand. "Without this, we'll never get them back…and you are just willing to throw your life away for nothing." She dropped his hand, walked over to her horse, and lifted her bow. "We should kill the wolf, and you should…what did you call it? Bind her spirit."

Tyr felt the red-hot anger reach his heart and boil to his voice. "No!" He stepped in front of Revna. "We came here to save her. If she is to die, it won't be by our hands." He yanked the pelt out of the pouch and stepped toward the wolf.

"I'll kill her if she takes one step toward you!" Revna called after. He heard her drawing an arrow.

Tyr approached and took in the size of the wolf and realized his mistake.

Growling erupted from the wolf's throat, and fur rose along her back. Her teeth were huge. The canine teeth overlapped the bottom jaw, and she showed no weakness at all, regardless of the blood loss and the bolts in her side. The wolf stood tall and faced Tyr. He was yards away and could feel he had overstepped his bounds.

He lifted the pelt before him, and a howl cut the air. He knelt and tossed the wolf pelt forward, and it glided between them, landing gracefully in the snow. The growl became a whimper, and he saw the wolf stumble and smell the pelt, its snarl returning, its eyes focused keenly on Tyr. The orange orbs glowed brightly as the gap closed between them.

He bowed his head and felt the hot breath upon his neck. He hadn't killed the wolf's son, but she didn't know that. He had brought the pelt home as directed by her pup. He could hear Revna behind him, and the bowstring was being drawn.

He waved his left hand, hoping she would see it and not shoot.

Quickly he reached up, yanked the bolt out of the wolf's neck, and moved to his right.

The jaws snapped on his left arm over the woven branches that protruded there, and he felt the canines sink into the skin beneath. The branches held firm against the wolf's jaw.

Then he fell to the snow, dropped by the wolf. She shook her head and grabbed the pelt, bringing it over to the other dead wolves, howling in grief over her loss.

Tyr breathed a deep sigh of relief. He had thought Revna was going to shoot the wolf when it struck him. He pushed out of the snow, dusting off his clothing. "See, that wasn't too bad."

Then he realized why Revna hadn't shot the wolf. Her bow lay in the snow, an arrow beside it. A great vine was entwined about her body, her mouth covered with leaves.

A hooded figure stood beside her, tall wooden staff in his left hand. Runes lined the wood. The figure wore a robe woven with leaves, something he had seen before. It looked like what Helena wore, like the leaves layering her bark skin. The hood was covered with feathers that formed a bird, and it draped to a point between the figure's eyes, which burned with green fire. His right hand was outstretched toward Revna, and the vines closed in around her. Tyr hadn't brought his weapons with him. He hadn't wanted to spook the wolf and had left them with his horse. He knew he was in trouble.

The voice under the hood spoke. "It's time for us to talk."

## Chapter 11: The Fenrix's Wrath

The wanderer walked away from Revna, the vines still entwined about her body, and made his way toward the wolf behind him. Revna struggled under the vines but couldn't break free.

Tyr thought he could make a run for his weapons and save her, then saw the vines tighten about her body.

"Walk with me," the wanderer said. He lowered his hand to his side, and the vines loosened about Revna. "The vines aren't hurting her, just confining her."

Tyr turned to walk with the wanderer. "Who are you?"

"I am from the Fenrix order. You may call me Axel," the wanderer told him as he approached the pups, then knelt beside them. "Such a pity."

The mother wolf approached and lay beside Axel, her head beside her pups. Tiny whimpers and labored breaths escaped her lips.

"Tell me, Vokter, do you intend to tether the souls of these pups to your will?" His eyes burned under the hood as he gazed upon Tyr.

"No," he replied, pointing to the pelt he had brought. "I came to bring her pup home."

"Was it not bound to you?"

"No. We killed the Vokter who had bound the pup

to him. I was asked to bring the pup home when I—"
Tyr stopped. "Enough with the questions. What do you
want from me, from us?"

"You're both Voktere, are you not?"

"No…only I am." He didn't feel confident in his
response. He gazed over at Revna wrapped in vines.
Her eyes went wide at his question.

"She hasn't told you?" Axel gazed at Tyr and stood
up. The green fires danced under the hood. "I can see
it in your eyes—you didn't know."

Tyr looked away from the green eyes under the
hood. Was Revna a Vokter? He hadn't even seen her call
any spirits or harness their abilities, had he? The
thoughts jumbled around as he went over the last
couple of days and even further into the past. They
would have found out long before the Warrior's Gate if
she was a Vokter.

The journey of the last day or two had shown him
that she was as interested in learning about tethering
and calling as he was. But nothing he thought of
proved Axel's case.

"She isn't a Vokter. I am." He stood resolute in his
words and faced Axel. "I would know."

"Believe as you will." He knelt beside the mother
wolf and whispered in her ear. The wolf howled, and
Tyr could feel her sorrow as he watched the wolf move

her head beside each pup and place her face in the snow. "Give me a moment to comfort a grieving mother."

Axel laid his staff in the snow, then lifted one of the pup's bodies and placed it beside the mother. His hands passed over the pup, and words passed through his lips. Then the ground shook beside the pup. Vines shot from the snow and wrapped gently around the pup's fallen form. Then the ground shifted and ebbed to engulf the pup. The mother wolf nuzzled her pup as the ground became whole once more.

The Fenrix Axel repeated the ritual for each fallen pup, and he brought the fur to the spot before the mother.

Tyr watched in awe as the Fenrix worked his magic to bury the pups. He had to wipe tears from his eyes at the carnage that had been done to this wolf's family. He saw the Fenrix place the pelt before the mother, and she nuzzled it. Then it hit him.

"Wait!" He rushed forward. The wolf, caught unaware, snarled and growled toward him. "Wait, please." His stretched out his hands to show he meant no harm.

"Yes?" Axel asked.

"May I hold the pelt for a moment?"

The Fenrix hesitated and whispered to the mother

wolf. The exchange was made, and the Fenrix passed Tyr the pelt near the mother's mouth.

Tyr reached forward slowly as the mother's keen eye followed him.

Then he proceeded to call to the pup. The wolf appeared before him and nodded. Tyr pointed to the others. The mother wolf had started to sniff around her but saw nothing. The Fenrix saw nothing as well.

*Please, Helena, help me—let this mother say goodbye to her pup. Please.* Tyr held the pelt before him and pleaded in his heart and mind. A tear rushed down his cheek. *Please.*

"*Fornyelse.*" The voice came to his mind, and he knew what to do. He reached out to place his hand upon the mother. She nipped as his hand landed upon her head. Then she stopped, her gaze focused upon her pup.

The mother wolf stood and moved forward. Tyr kept his hand upon her and his mind on the wolf's pelt.

"*Mother*" The wolf pup moved forward and nuzzled his mother.

Tyr watched as the mother and pup shared a moment. Wolfish growls and howls were exchanged between them. He watched as the mother lowered herself to be near her pup and placed her head near it. They comforted each other, then the pup howled and rushed away.

Tyr could see where the wolf's tears had fallen to the snow as she raised her head and gazed toward Tyr, his hand still upon her.

"Sorry." He moved his hand.

The mother wolf stood erect before him and bowed her head. Then she moved back to her original position. Tyr waited for her to settle before handing the pelt back to the Fenrix.

"Interesting." The Fenrix grabbed the pelt and performed the burial. Then the mother howled for each pup that had been buried at her side. She laid her head into the snow, eyes closing, her breathing heavy.

The Fenrix walked a little way from the wolf toward the cave's mouth, staff in hand, waving Tyr to follow.

"These wolves are rare in the world. There are not many left," the Fenrix said as Tyr stepped beside. "To lose her, so many of her kind…" He turned to face the wolf. "Nature grieves."

Tyr looked at the wolf. Her body had stood right at his height, nearly six feet tall. Muscles were pronounced through the thick blue fur, which was covered in specks of blood and matted to her side. Her tail looked at least as long as his arm, from his vantage point. "What kind of wolf is she?"

"A dire wolf." His voice came out with respect

pressed upon the words, and he bowed his head. "She shall be sorely missed."

Tyr looked over, trying to see if she had any wounds he hadn't noticed prior. "Can't we save her, patch up those wounds?"

"It's the heart that cannot be mended."

He realized it then. The streaks matted her fur around the eyes. She was grieving the loss of her young ones. Helplessness wasn't anything Tyr liked to feel. That feeling that he could do nothing to help this glorious beast survive another day. Without her young, she had already given up the fight and will to live.

"You're beginning to understand why I am here," Axel said, tapping his staff against Tyr's shoulder.

The touch of his staff sent the immediate fight-or-flight reaction through his body, and he decided to fight. "Why are you here? For me to watch you bury this wolf's children? To hold Revna hostage while you show me this wolf's pain?"

"My wrath is why I came here. I came to put an end to all those causing harm to nature's creatures." His eyes burned brighter, and Tyr saw the vines twist tighter around Revna, her eyes going wide in panic. "To end the suffering caused to the creatures that call to me."

Tyr felt the vines latch upon his foot and move up his leg. He tried to step away and tripped into the snow.

He tried to turn his body, feeling the vines forcing their way up. Panic set in as Tyr realized he was helpless. He reached down to harness Kanin.

His wits became very keen, and he saw his surroundings very visible then. "I am not like them," he called to Axel.

The vines tugged against him, then brought his body upward, wrapping about him. His face was now in line with the Fenrix as the vine reached his neck. "I know."

"Let me—" Leaves popped from the vines and covered his mouth.

"No, let me be clear. My wrath doesn't stop here. If you take one step out of line or go down a path like the enforcing Voktere did, I'll kill you where you stand. Understood?" The vines tightened about Tyr as he nodded. It was becoming harder to breathe within the vines. They were constricting his chest. He heard a howl escape the mother wolf's lips, then he fell to the snow upon his knees. The vines fell away and slithered back into the snowy earth.

Then the Fenrix continued. "The wolf grieves for her pups." He turned and walked to the wolf, placing his hand upon her head where she lay. "What you did for her before is why she wishes to return the favor, and she has asked that I allow her to accompany you."

"Isn't she dying?" Tyr asked, gazing upon the Fenrix

and wolf.

"To be tethered…to your kind." The Fenrix spoke slowly and in disgust. "I've been watching you and have seen into your heart. I see what you could become as well." He stepped toward Tyr and made sure their eyes locked before speaking. "One step out of line, and my wrath shall fall upon you." With those words, he pointed his staff, and a gust of wind and snow knocked Tyr onto his backside. Then the Fenrix was gone.

"Tyr!" Revna's voice came from behind him. "Where did he go?"

"I don't know." He looked around, finding no sign of him.

"Are you good?" she asked, helping him to his feet.

Tyr rubbed his chest where the vines had pressed in. "I'm good. Not sure how much more my chest can take before it's permanently bruised, though."

"I'm just glad you are safe." She threw her arms around him. It had been a long time since she had done that, and he threw his arms around her too.

"We're both safe now," he reassured her.

The wolf let out one last howl, and then her head crashed into the snow, tongue lolling out of her mouth.

Tyr let Revna go and moved to the wolf's side, helping close her mouth to give her peace. "Not sure I can do it," he said out loud.

"Do what?"

"Skin this great animal and make a totem." He looked up at Revna. "Do you know how much pain I've already caused, and what I'm going to cause to everyone who thought they knew me?"

"What are you talking about?"

"I'm a Vokter. Just a couple of days ago, that meant nothing but history to me. Now here I am skinning beasts to tether their spirits to this realm. How sick and twisted is that?"

Revna said nothing as Tyr paced.

"I am going to save a family that will disown me as soon as they find out who I am. Njal won't let me live in the village after this is done. Or will I even make it home alive?" He fell to his knees.

Revna moved to his side. "We need to get moving if we're going to save anyone. It's nearly sunset."

Tyr looked around him and could see the night settling in. He felt annoyed that Revna was always in a rush to have Tyr meet his end. Annoyed as he was, he made his way to his horse and pulled out his skinning knife, then approached the wolf. "Then we'd better get this over with."

Tyr skinned the wolf and removed its teeth and claws,

and then they took off into the night, riding in silence. They headed north toward Eski, which was another day's journey, and stopped when it became too dark to continue.

They made camp without a word to one another. Tyr hadn't made himself approachable during the ride when Revna had reached out to talk. He made sure she knew he still wasn't in the mood to talk about any of it.

Skinning the wolf and removing her claws and teeth had been a grueling effort for him. Each time he had done it while out on the hunt had been different. This beast had been different, and he had choked back tears while performing the act.

He laid the furs out around him by the firelight and started to organize them into different designs from the length of fur he had gathered—cloak, gloves, and others. He went through a handful more before Revna approached.

"You should make a shoulder pad out of her paw and claws," she said over his shoulder, looking down at what he had laid out.

Annoyed as he was with her, he knew she was right. He gathered the paw and claws together and lifted them to his right shoulder. "Like this?"

"Oh yeah! Looks amazing." She moved a few of the claws around on top of his shoulder. "Perfect."

He lowered the fur back to the ground, the claws falling about. He piled them together. "I have a question for you," he said.

"Yeah?" she said, a smile on her face. "What's on your mind?"

Tyr had thought about what Axel said about her being a Vokter. It had been part of why he was annoyed with her. Had she hidden the fact that she was one? "Did you hear what he said about you?"

"Who?"

"The Fenrix."

"Oh." The smile faded, and she moved to the other side of the fire. "Yeah, and I heard what you said back."

"Are you a Vokter?" he came right out and asked. There was no reason to hold back anymore. They were heading into enemy territory where they would be the enemy.

"Well…" she started.

"Are you, or are you not?"

"Yes, but don't be mad at me," she said quickly.

Her words hit him, and all rational thought went out the window. "I had no reason to believe that you were. Why did you hide it from me after all that we have been through together?"

"I thought that—"

"That I would be mad?" He stood up and looked at

her, pain in his voice. "I thought I was alone in all of this, and the entire time you already knew how to tether and were just going along with it…just like Erik did." He turned and walked away.

"I don't know how…was never taught that way," Revna said quietly.

Tyr turned to face her as she focused on the snow melting away by the fire. "What do you mean?"

"I took their wills away from them." She glanced up and unbuckled the leather strap about her arm, letting it fall away. There was fur beneath it to keep her warm, and then Tyr saw runes glow upon it.

A fox appeared beside her, gazing at her, then at Tyr. "I took this poor spirit's will away from her." She reached down and rubbed the top of the fox's head. "When you started to show me another way to bind the spirits, I had to learn what you knew. I watched and observed, then the other night I untethered the fox from myself and bound it willingly, giving her a name." She stood up and buckled the leather tightly around her arm again, and the fox dissipated into mist. "I even hid anything that would give me away."

Tyr still had no words to say. Even just seeing her call the fox left him dumbfounded. He wasn't the only one. She was a Vokter. He rushed forward and threw his arms around her. "I thought I was alone." He tried to swallow the knot in his throat as he spoke. "I hate being alone."

She embraced him back. "You're not alone anymore."

After they finished hugging each other, Tyr went back to the furs. "We have so much we can teach each other and learn as we go."

"Precisely," she exclaimed. "Now let's make this shoulder pad and give your wolf a name. Then we can talk some more. I want to know more about what you are learning and how to do it." She rushed over to help him create the totem.

"Okay," he said as they pulled the furry paw and claws together.

Tyr sat beside the fire holding the large paw, its claws still attached, before him. He called to the dire wolf.

The wolf appeared beside the firelight, paws pressed into the snow, then she nodded. "*Thank you for giving me time with my child*," the wolf said in his mind.

"*It was the least I could do. Axel said that it was your wish to tether so you can continue your journey here in the mortal realm?*" he asked the wolf back.

The wolf nodded. "*I seek vengeance, and I owe you a blood debt for saving my life and bringing my child to me.*"

"*Then I shall tether you to your mortal body until your debt has been paid. Do you have a name?*"

*"Catori."* The wolf then howled.

Tyr wove the runes into the fur, then completed the ritual as the wolf departed.

Revna and Tyr grabbed additional leather, slicing it into strips to bind the paw to Tyr's shoulder.

"How does it look?" Tyr asked, turning the large paw upon his right shoulder so that the claws dipped down menacingly.

"Intimidating. Though you've always been."

He stopped and looked at her. "Always?"

"Get over it. No matter how hard anyone pushed you, you always came out on top. Never let failure get in your way. Was hard for the rest of us to keep up with you. Well, I guess not so much for me." She smiled as she crossed to the other side of the fire and prepared a place to sleep.

"Just never heard you say it that way. Feels nice." Tyr walked to his bedding. "Intimidating. I like the sound of that."

He felt the snowball hit him across the back of his head. He reached down, grabbed a handful of snow, then turned to throw it at her.

A figure moved quickly toward Revna, and Tyr dropped the snowball. "Watch out!"

Revna turned and found a shield smashing against her face, dropping her to the ground.

Tyr reached down for his shield and axe to face the intruder as the light hit his face. Njal.

"Njal? What are you doing?" Tyr lowered his shield as Njal stepped over Revna's still body.

"It all makes sense now." He stepped around the fire, his axe and shield in his hands. "You led them to the village to kill us…after all these years…traitors in our midst."

"You aren't making any sense. What are you talking about?" Tyr lifted his shield and stepped back into a defensive posture. "You're losing your mind. Erik was the traitor, not me."

"Erik isn't a Vokter. You and she are." He looked from Revna to Tyr as he spoke and continued forward. "This time I'll make sure there are no Voktere left in the world when I'm through."

Tyr realized Njal wasn't thinking right. He had to get through to him. He dropped his shield and lifted his left hand. "I have the relic. We can get our people back. We found it and brought it to get our people back."

"Our people? You aren't one of us, you traitor. I'll take the relic off your cold dead body and get *my* people back." He rushed forward, axe aimed at Tyr's head. Tyr had let his guard down by dropping his shield. He ducked, moving to the side, and found Njal's knee colliding with his chin.

Tyr fell to his backside and looked up to see Njal's foot slam into his chest. The wind left his body, and he was knocked onto his back. Njal, foot still on his chest, kicked Tyr's axe aside. Tyr thought of calling Catori, but he didn't want to cause Njal any more pain than he was already feeling, so he stopped just before calling her.

Footsteps rushed into the camp, and Tyr saw Erik, Odger, and Gertrude surround their campground. The pain of seeing Erik approach was enough to set Tyr's heart amiss. The man who had betrayed him just the other day. Erik averted his gaze.

"Tie him up along with her. We'll need to make an example of these two when we get back home." Njal spat upon Tyr's face and growled, "I should have never accepted you as a Kriger."

# Chapter 12: An Unfortunate Reunion

Tyr's hands were tied in front of him. His belongings had been removed, along with the totems. Njal had searched Revna closely and removed anything that looked like it could be a totem, then had her strap the leather armor on before he tied her hands. Odger asked Njal to destroy the totems, but he declined, saying they had to be destroyed appropriately or karma would harm their people. Odger had started to press the point, mentioning demons, but Njal shut down the conversation, saying it was over.

Odger had been commissioned to remove the relic from Tyr's hand, but no such luck. Each time Odger broke off a wooden tendril, another grew to replace it.

Eventually Tyr gave up trying to explain himself to Njal and the other Krigere. It hurt to be in such a spot where the family he'd once had was now neglecting him.

Revna had a large bruise on the side of her face from where the shield had clipped her. She kept her hair covering her face as much as she could, not wanting to look or talk to anyone, while the Krigere began to make camp. Njal made sure to keep Tyr and Revna from each other, placing them on opposite sides of the camp.

"Any luck?" Njal asked as Odger cut another tendril,

which was quickly replaced by a new one. Tyr winced, knowing the pain was coming.

"Can't remove the blasted thing. It replaces itself faster than I can break it." He broke two tendrils quickly and watched them grow back as soon as he had broken them. "Even trying to block them from reentering his skin was impossible. They found a way around, then moved back into place. Should we remove his hand?"

"No need. We'll hand them both over when we get there." Njal turned to walk away.

"Let me help," Tyr said, hoping to catch Njal before he left. "Please."

Njal stopped, then walked close to Tyr's face. "I would die before I asked for your help, boy."

"They have my mor, Liv," Tyr pleaded. "Let me help bring her home."

Njal gnashed his teeth. "We don't need your help, just that contraption on your hand." He walked away.

Tyr pulled his hand away from Odger, calling after Njal, "Why do you hate the Voktere so much?"

He stopped and lowered his head. "There are things you will never understand." There was pain in his voice.

"Try me."

Njal looked up at Tyr. "No." Then he left Odger alone with Tyr.

"What is wrong with him?" Tyr asked Odger.

No reply. Odger picked up his tools and walked away. No matter how Tyr asked or spoke to them, he was ignored.

What had caused Njal to hate the Voktere? The question rolled through his mind. It went back to the history of the Kriger and Vokter conflict. The war had been because of the enforcers breaking the code and enslaving the spirits to their will. Once the two had worked in harmony, but then it started. There had to be others who hadn't followed in the footsteps of the enforcers and who knew what Tyr knew now about tethering the spirits and allowing free will to continue. There was an itch that he couldn't ignore. Njal knew something Tyr didn't, and it was bothering him. Revna would know more than he did about the history, but they had been separated.

He had wanted to talk with Revna in the morning after he had found out she was a Vokter but hadn't wanted to press the point. Now they were stuck in an unfortunate situation with people who no longer accepted them.

Tyr closed his eyes, anger very present in his mind. Sleep eventually grasped hold as he tried to stay warm in the cold night.

"Fornyelse." The voice warmed his heart as he approached the sanctuary where Helena sat pleasantly on the bench, awaiting his arrival. "Welcome, Tyr." She smiled as he stepped into the sanctuary and settled upon the bench next to her.

He could see the lush oasis of greenery. Water flowed gently down the rocks behind Helena. There were small fish in the pond, and a tree grew beside the water. The place looked more alive than in previous trips here.

"We're prisoners now." Tyr sighed. "My people found us, bound us, and removed all of the totems we made."

"We?" she asked, curiosity in her voice.

"Forgot to tell you—Revna is a Vokter like me." Tyr's spirits rose and fell as he spoke. "Found out right…well, before we were ambushed."

"Interesting facts. You're a prisoner, your friend is a Vokter…Anything else?"

Tyr thought about when he had last spoken with Helena, then caught her up. He talked about the Fenrix he had met, along with the wolf and her pups, how he'd untethered the totems from the spirits, been knocked flat trying to harness Kanin, and tethered to the dire wolf.

Helena nodded during the breakdown of what had occurred since their last meeting. When Tyr had finished, she brought her hand to her mouth to cover a smile. "You've been doing just fine without all my leskes, though I should mention the totem reserves. Check the reserves before you harness or call to them. You got the psychic feedback from the totem that had no reserve."

"I'd be dead without your leskes. Without your guidance I never would have made it this far," he responded. "Revna was trying to learn what you had been teaching me. She enforced the spirits to her will but had begun to unravel her totems, allowing the spirits to have their will back. Those leskes you taught me are helping more than just me."

Helena nodded, lowering her hand to reveal the smile. "You're calm, child."

Tyr realized that he had been. The whole time, he hadn't been angry or vengeful. He'd told it as it was to Helena, and he saw that the darkness hadn't ebbed into the sanctuary. "You're right."

"Magical." She waved her hands. "Fornyelse."

He felt the wave of warmth flow through his body, and his mind relished the relief. "Every time you say that word, I feel renewed strength and hope and the will to continue. It calms my anger and allows me to focus. What have you been doing?"

"My purpose, child. To teach you the leskes I promised a long time ago." She lowered her head. "It was their wish for me to protect you and teach you the proper ways of the Voktere."

"Whose wish was that?"

"That time has yet to reveal itself."

Tyr felt the slight edge in his mind. She was stalling, and he didn't like it. "When will it be time?"

She didn't respond right away but moved off the bench and over to the tree beside the pond, pressing her hand against it. "Patience, child. These gifts of yours are growing step by step. Rushing the course only leads toward darkness." Her other hand waved at the darkness outside the sanctuary. "When you entered this place, the darkness followed. I've been tasked with renewing your mind, your soul, and who you are to become."

Tyr stood up, his patience wearing thin. "You're speaking in riddles now."

"Nonsense." She turned toward him. The darkness crept in. "Guidance, child. Were I to share all of my knowledge with you, you would fall. It has to come when you are ready and willing to know more."

"I am willing!" He stepped forward. "There is so much I don't understand anymore. I thought I knew... who I was. An orphan with no parents besides Liv. Grew up with two things in mind: one, to become the best Kriger ever known, and two, to unravel my past.

Now it's just a blur. I grew up being betrayed and lied to, the mor who raised me is now captive to a man who wants this relic, and I don't even know why."

"Oh, child," Helena said softly near the tree. "All shall be revealed in due time."

"I don't think I can wait any longer." Tyr lowered his head, tears upon his face.

Silence passed between them for a moment, then the ground shook in the sanctuary.

"We've run out of time. Listen closely to what I am about to tell you." She stepped toward Tyr, the ground shaking as she went. As her hand rested on his shoulder, she continued. "They're trying to remove the relic again. They cannot take it from you. It is not time to reveal the details to you. You must travel to Mork Skog. There you'll find wisdom enough for us to continue the leskes." The ground shook, and darkness flowed farther in. "Do you understand?"

"No!" He tried to keep his footing as the ground shook. The riddles in Helena's words kept confusing him.

"Protect the relic and find wisdom in Mork Skog!" Her eyes blazed green as the darkness swallowed them up.

Tyr opened his eyes to the stinging pain of Odger and Njal pulling at the relic and cutting the strands. Blood dripped from his hand from where they had nicked his skin repeatedly as they tried to remove the tendrils. He pulled his hands away and felt Njal's strength keeping him there.

"Remove it!" Njal yelled.

"Almost there." Odger was prying and ripping the tendrils apart, blocking their access to Tyr's skin for reentry.

"Stop!" Tyr screamed in pain as they forced the relic from his hand. Then the air collapsed around them. Njal and Odger were knocked back from the force, and the tendrils moved their way into his skin.

"Fornyelse." He heard the words in his mind as the wounds upon his skin started to close.

"Tuller du!" Njal slammed his fist into the snow. "Glem det. Let's move out. We're going with our initial plan."

Odger picked himself up off the ground and pulled Tyr to his feet. "Get up and move."

Tyr got to his feet and moved where Odger was taking him. They approached the horses and forced Tyr onto the back of one. Then Odger got on behind him.

"Let me go!" he heard Revna yell and saw her knock Erik to the side, then run.

Njal pounced on top of her and knocked her to the ground, where she struggled. Erik arrived and helped Njal stop Revna from kicking so much. They held her down for a moment.

"Knock it off. You're going with us!" He grabbed her tied hands and yanked her off the ground. They brought her to the horse beside Tyr. Njal got Revna on the horse, then saddled behind her.

Tyr glanced over and saw Revna hide her face. "You okay?"

"No talking!" Odger slammed his fist into the back of Tyr's head.

Tyr caught the occasional glance from Revna and Erik as they rode in silence.

They stopped a handful of times, and then Odger switched with Erik. Tyr made sure to push Erik off the horse as he climbed up and to call him a traitor, which earned him a few more knocks to the head. Erik decided to ride his horse next to Tyr's, pulling Tyr's horse beside his.

The ride north brought them farther into the cold weather, and the snow started to fall heavily. Fur coverings had been provided to all the riders to preserve their body heat as the cold and the heavy snowfall settled around them.

"I want to explain why," Erik said as he threw the fur about Tyr's shoulders.

"I don't care what you have to say, Erik. You led me into a trap and left me there to die," Tyr spit toward Erik. "Glemme deg!"

Erik walked away and hopped on his horse, and they continued to ride north toward Eski.

Erik slowed their horses for a moment, then got closer to Tyr. "Think what you will, but they took my family and said if I didn't bring you there, then they were going to kill them."

When he heard Erik start to speak, he had wanted to spit at him again, but then he stopped. Erik's family had been taken before the morning? Why hadn't he just told Tyr instead of leading him into a trap? "We should have figured it out together," he responded.

"We couldn't have. It was all so quick. I don't know how they got inside the walls, but when I got home after the celebration, a man approached me and told me what I had to do," Erik whispered. "If I informed anyone, he said, they would execute my family on the spot. Sorry, I didn't have a choice."

"You always have a choice!" Tyr let the anger settle in his voice. "We've known each other our entire lives. I would have done anything to save your family. You were like a brother to me, and I don't think I'll ever trust you again."

Erik stuttered a word, then stopped.

Tyr remembered whom they had taken. Erik's family had been among those who had not turned up dead but were missing from the village.

Tyr had been caught up in the Voktere, and being one himself, he had forgotten why they had journeyed north in the first place. They not only had Liv but Berner and Elsie, the two children who had played with his axe and shield during the celebration. Then other members of the Krigere had been among the missing.

"I'm sorry," Tyr said to Erik. "We're—" Then he realized that his hands were still tied and remembered he was a prisoner and not part of the rescue plan. "Njal will get them back for you."

"Thanks for the hope. We've been missing that lately." Erik sped their horses to catch up with the others. Tyr could see Njal had turned to see where they had gone.

Tyr knew that they still had a long way before them.

Njal ordered them to stop as the sun dipped over the horizon, leaving a blazing orange glow upon it.

Tyr looked to see where they were and could see the

village off in the distance below them. Eski. They had traveled closer to the mountains to look down into the valley. It was a perfect position. Njal had led them right to the place where they could spot the village from a safe distance.

People moved about the village ruins, which had been built in a circle surrounded by mounds of dirt and stone, with three major entry points, south, east, and west. The backside of the village led into the large waters beyond.

Creatures with a light-blue glow surrounding their bodies followed the guards around the perimeter. Nature had taken back the village, and the overgrowth covered the roofs and grounds inside.

Tyr couldn't make out who the people were and where the hostages were positioned in the village, and the light was diminishing quickly. They moved farther away and set camp without fire that night.

"They are going to be dead weight!" Odger shouted.

"I understand your frustration, old friend," Njal responded. "But we can't just leave them here and hope to find them when we get back. And Gorm wants the relic."

Odger grumbled, but others chimed in to agree with Njal.

Njal had to calm the other Krigere down, even his

daughter Gertrude. Erik remained silent throughout the process.

"We need the extra hands!" Gertrude said. "Regardless of how we feel about Tyr and Revna, they are some of the best we've got." Other Krigere shifted in place. "No offense," she offered.

"They can't be trusted!" came a shout.

"Their kind killed my friends," shouted another.

"Calm down and prepare for the battle ahead of us." Njal stood and moved to the center. "When you are constantly fighting the battle behind us for those we've lost, you'll never win the fight. We fight now for those we can still bring home. We need our rest for the night. During our travels here, I've clarified what the Voktere are capable of and taught many of you how to fight them.

"During the day we leave ourselves open to be spotted by the enemy and lose the element of surprise. It's going to be a long day tomorrow, my fellow Krigere. We do not fear that death will stop us from what we fight for. Let us remember our kinship has brought us this far and shall persist long after we're dead. Rest easy and let us use our knowledge to fight the odds against us. This scourge that has plagued our people will be stamped out of existence tomorrow night. Don't let your anger and fear consume you today."

He sat down then and continued to eat his food. Others settled down and moved to their areas to sleep, while a few kept watch.

Tyr heard them discuss invading Eski the following night to keep from being seen. They would make their way around in two separate groups. Then the conversations started to wind down and became common talk.

Tyr never got the chance to talk to anyone. They kept ignoring any pleas or comments he made during dinner. They moved Revna away after they fed her. They moved Tyr after he finished eating.

They tied him to a tree near the sleeping Krigere. He saw Revna on her side facing away from him, also tied by a rope to a nearby tree.

"Revna," he whispered. "Revna, are you awake?"

She stirred and rolled to face him, then brushed her hair aside. "Yeah."

"How are you?"

"Eh." She shrugged her shoulders.

"We need to get out of here." Tyr pulled at the ropes around his wrists and chest.

"No use trying." She raised her hands out of the furs to show the bruising along her wrists. "Tried all day to break the ropes. Without my Fylgja, I'm useless."

He hadn't heard that word before. "Fylgja?"

Revna opened her eyes a little wider, then laughed. "Gosh, you never studied at all, you half-troll. Fylgjur is what the Voktere call their spirits. Funny that it comes up now."

Tyr let out a laugh as he thought about the history of the Voktere. Fylgja seemed like a word he would likely remember. Then again, reading just wasn't his thing. He had skimmed a lot of the text, trying to get it over with.

"Sorry it turned out like this," Tyr said after a good silent laugh.

"Wasn't your fault." She pulled the furs closer about her and up to her chin. "Never expected to stay in Kjarra forever. Knew my time would come to leave."

Tyr thought about her words. He had thought the same thing just the other day during the celebration. He felt he had learned all he needed in Kjarra. Becoming an official Kriger was his last step before diving into his past. "I know what you mean. Doesn't mean we had to leave on such bad terms, though. If we ever leave at all."

The camp had settled down for the night. Conversations became few, and snores and animals became the major source of sound around the camp. An occasional howl, hoot, or crunching of nature became pleasing to the ear.

His hand throbbed from where they had nicked him earlier that day. What was unique about the relic they had found? It looked simple, a small wooden rectangle with wooden tendrils around it. It had caused much trouble the last couple of days. His life had been turned upside down overnight, and it was all coming crashing down upon him.

Would Liv accept him, and would Njal give him a chance to say goodbye to her? The pressure upon his chest over the heart made him realize the pain he was going through. It would be hard to tell her about who he was becoming and that he was going to set out to find his past.

Being determined made it easier to reach the goals ahead of him. Obstacles or roadblocks had been before him, then became distant objects in the past. He ached for Liv and being welcomed home each night by a loving mor who accepted him. The ropes became tight against his wrists, toying with the thoughts in his mind, making it difficult to focus on his present condition.

They had to get out of here. Liv needed him. Njal and the others needed their help if they were to save the hostages. He needed to get them out of this mess.

"You awake?" he asked quietly.

"No," came the quiet reply from Revna.

"Any ideas how to get out of here? I've got nothing."

Tyr had tried to pry the ropes off, yank them, and break them by rubbing them together, and it had gotten him nowhere.

"Going to figure it out in the morning," Revna said confidently.

"Oh, good thinking." Tyr had thought the best time to escape would be while the others were sleeping. But the chaos of the morning might give them the chance to escape. He lay down, staring up at the cloudy sky.

"Tyr," a voice whispered beside him.

He pushed himself up and whispered back, "Who's there?"

"Erik," the voice responded. "Be ready in the morning."

"For what?"

"I've got a plan. Be ready," Erik said, and Tyr heard crunching snow as Erik returned to camp. He didn't trust Erik, but with his hands tied, Tyr wasn't going anywhere without help.

# Chapter 13: The Betrayer's Rescue

Tyr fell asleep a short while after Erik said he had a plan. Only hours passed before he felt himself having to force his eyes open. Erik tapped him lightly, pressing a finger to his lips to keep him quiet.

The stars gave what light they could. Clouds moved in from the east, bringing another snowfall.

It was catching up to Tyr, the lack of sleep, constant strain, and fighting. When the ropes were cut, he shook his hands and moved the ropes away from his body. Then he rubbed his eyes, forcing himself awake. Revna sat up, pushing the ropes away from her body and dusting off the snow that had fallen upon her furs.

"Don't touch me," she told Erik quietly as he tried to help her up.

Erik turned to Tyr, reaching out a hand. The moment passed between them, and Tyr reached up, grasping his hand. "Doesn't change things."

"I know. Follow me and be quiet." Erik tiptoed around the trees away from the camp.

Once they had cleared the grove where the Krigere had made camp, they ducked behind rocks to avoid any of the watchmen.

"Let's stop here for a moment before moving on." Erik sat against a rock and slid down. "Need to ask both of you a favor."

Tyr and Revna glanced at one another. Tyr knelt in the snow, and Revna stood with her arms folded.

"A favor?" Revna asked. "Guess I do owe you one for saving our lives back there. Can't speak for Tyr though."

Tyr played with the snow, glancing at Erik. "We're even now. Anything I do now, I do of my own free will."

Erik nodded to them. "Your belongings are covered by a mound of snow. I'll take you to them after I explain my favor, and you can do as you will." Erik started to wipe the sweat from his head. These situations had always made Erik nervous, which showed in his nervous twitching and movements.

Revna tapped her foot impatiently. "Go on."

"We need your help down there. The Voktere we encountered on our way here took a toll on our numbers and mental state. Njal has pressed them forward regardless of their questions. It's been for the sake of their loved ones that they even press on.

"Without the both of you, we're sorely outnumbered, and I'm worried that it won't matter when we save the hostages if so many of our own have lost their lives in the process. That's why I took your belongings and am asking that you help save our loved ones. Please."

Revna spoke first. "Erik, did you see what they just did to us? They don't want our help."

"I know, but it isn't about their pride and arrogance. It's our loved ones down there who are going to suffer," Erik pleaded. He waved toward Eski, invisible from their vantage point.

Tyr agreed with Revna. There wasn't a point to fighting alongside the Krigere when they had treated them as prisoners, traitors to their own. The logic was sound in how the last day had played itself out in his mind. It was time to cut ties and move on. But his heart and soul felt different. These people were his family.

"I agree with Revna...however, I'll help." Tyr lifted his left hand to Erik. The relic showed in the twilight. "Gorm wants this. Let's give him what he wants and get out to fight another day. If we can make it down there before Njal, we can end it before it begins."

"After all they just put you through, you're going to just hand the relic over and hope that Njal forgets who we are?" Revna was irritated, shifting her body side to side, arms crossed.

"Never said I'd go back home after—he made that very clear to me. Erik can bring the hostages back to Njal after we hand the relic over to Gorm, and we'll leave," Tyr responded.

"You want me to...go down there with you?" Erik

asked nervously.

"It's the only way you can get the others safely back to Njal without him bringing us back with him." Tyr got up off his knees.

"Erik, thanks for freeing us, but the favor you're asking is insane," Revna said. "Take me to my things and let me decide what I want to do. This won't be a favor I will be accepting." Revna said.

Erik had no reply. They had been friends long enough that he knew when Revna put her foot down like that, he wasn't going to change her mind with pleading. Tyr knew that. She had made up her mind, and that was that.

They moved from the rock and made their way south away from Eski to a large formation of stones surrounded by trees. The trees leaned around the stones to reach the sunlight, and the snow was heavy atop the stones, with sharp edges jutting out.

Erik kicked the snow between the stones to reveal their belongings under the fur he had covered them with.

"Better watch our backs, Tyr," she said, rushing to her things. "I'll get ready, and then we'll swap."

"Toss me my axe and shield at least. Don't take forever," he said.

"Boys," she said, tossing his axe and shield over to

him, then started to set her totems back into place.

Erik stood with his axe and shield at the ready. Tyr adjusted the straps and set his stance.

"Do you honestly think Njal can't handle it with the group of Krigere he has?" Tyr wondered if Erik truly felt that they couldn't succeed and had to be sure.

"We struggled with the last group we ran into. We lost four and had to bury them and continue." Erik shook his head. "The creatures that they summon…"

"Fylgjur," Revna corrected.

"Whatever. We were ready to fight double or triple our numbers along with those beasts."

"Fylgjur," she said again.

"Just get ready!" Erik shouted. Tyr smiled. It was just like the good old days, except different. "Njal described the totems we were looking for and how ignoring the beasts—Fylgjur—would make them disappear after we took out the Voktere who had summoned them. It just wasn't enough to get past a troll, bear, and wolf."

"Njal should have warned us that the Voktere were not all gone," Tyr said. "When we talked about meeting one, it felt exciting. Now I am one of them, and I am confused. Even Revna is one of them. Njal just exiled us on the spot, no answers to why."

"I know." Erik bowed his head. "They interrogated me after they found me. Left some decent marks on me.

Njal wanted to know why I had betrayed you and why I was working for Gorm. I tried to explain that I didn't know anyone by the name of Gorm, and how they had said they would leave my family alone if I brought them to you. Regardless of what I told Njal, he made me remove all my clothing down to my briefs, making sure no totems were present." Erik looked at Tyr. "He thought I was one of them. Asked me a slew of questions that I had no answers to and made sure I didn't lie." He tried to pry his leather up around his stomach to reveal a couple of day-old bruises.

Tyr winced at the bruises. "After we're done getting our loved ones back, I hope I get the chance to tell you what I went through the last couple of days."

Revna passed by then, lifting one hand in front of her, showing the bruises left from the ropes. In her other hand, she held her shield. "Left some good ones on me too, and one day I'll get payback. Tyr, go get your things. I'll take watch."

"On it." Tyr dropped his watchful gaze, then turned back to get his things. He tossed his shield to the ground beside the fur, then pulled the cover off. There was nothing there.

"Drop your weapons!" shouted a loud voice.

He turned back toward Revna and Erik to find armed men pointing crossbows at them. One was atop the rock, aiming down. The other was behind Revna, crossbow at the ready. Revna's hands were in the air, shield on the ground. Erik was still holding his axe and shield and was facing Revna.

"Turn around!" another voice shot from behind Tyr. He turned to find another man standing before him, his dark brown hair tied in a ponytail, sword pointed before him, and a spirit wolf who looked like the pups from the other day—the Vokter's Fylgja. Instantly Tyr's eyes narrowed on the troll hide on his arm.

Tyr hadn't grabbed his axe and shield from the ground when he had heard the shouting. He was unarmed.

They had been betrayed again. Tyr had worried that Erik was leading them into a trap, and now he was sure of it.

He started to lower himself to his knees. He was still a good few feet from his axe and shield. The wolf snarled and moved forward between the stones, the man close behind.

"No fear of death!" Tyr roared the Kriger virtue. He got hold of his axe as the wolf dashed toward him.

He arced his axe upward at the wolf's lunge, catching it under the neck. The claws raked his arms, leaving streaks of blood as the wolf disappeared into the mist.

The sword gleamed above his head, and he brought

his aching axe arm up to parry it.

The weapons clashed, and the sword dipped down and sliced his hand. The axe dropped into the snow, and Tyr started to move back on his hands.

Blood dotted the snow as he scuffled backward. The claws that had raked against his skin and his now-bloody hand throbbed under his weight.

A smile rose upon the man's face as he walked toward Tyr, his sword dipped to skewer him.

"Stop!" cried a woman's voice. "He is needed alive."

Tyr turned to see the man with the crossbow unconscious on the ground. Erik was on the ground; a bolt protruded from the side of his chest.

Revna stepped past the bodies, pushed aside the man's sword at Tyr's chest, and knelt before Tyr. Her beautiful blond hair cascaded along her feminine features, her blue eyes locked with his, and his heart panicked.

"I'm going to need that relic now," she said as Tyr felt his world crumbling around him.

# Chapter 14: Ravens

The grace of the clouds brought their light snow, and morning light broke over the eastern horizon, light refracting off each flake that fell to the earth below.

Tyr felt the cold beneath his hands, the pain muffled between numb fingers and the frost gathering around him. But nothing compared to how he looked at the woman who had been his close companion and friend. Missing sections of the puzzle forming in his mind made it hard to focus on the beautiful blue-eyed blonde standing over him. Her lips were pursed together as she awaited an answer, her eyes focused intently on him. No anger could resolve the torment in his heart.

"Revna." Tyr parted his cold lips to form the only words he could. "Why?"

She made a slight twist of her face, blinking to accept the words. Then a cold stare of resolve formed, and she focused back on him. "Why hope for an ending that cannot possibly happen? Njal was blinded by anger toward the Voktere, and when I found my true purpose, it was just a matter of time before my secret was revealed," she said. "All these years my mor had kept it from me, lied to protect me from Njal's pathetic judgment. After she passed, I found a note she had written about the nature of my far, a Vokter."

Revna wiped a tear from her face, continuing, "She told me she was sorry for never telling me about my far and said I may have Vokter blood running in my veins." She lay her shield on the snow. Dim blue light rose from her hair, and a raven appeared, covered with a Fylgja's blue illumination. "I never had a proper mentor to teach me about the Voktere and the abilities we possessed."

The raven glided around her head while a dim blue light appeared again under her hair. Another raven appeared and circled about her head.

"Then I found Gorm and his henchmen, and they taught me what it meant to be a Vokter." She reached her hand out. "Give me your hand."

Tyr moved back in the snow, away from Revna and the ravens. "No. It doesn't have to be this way."

"It does." She stood. The runes flared under her leather armor. A giant serpent slithered through the snow before Tyr. His eyes went wide. "Ah, you remember the serpent's sister."

Tyr tried to get away, shuffling to his feet. The serpent slithered forward and wrapped its body quickly around him. The shadowed remembrance of pain echoed through his body, and he screamed, feeling slight pulses throughout his body.

The serpent wound about his body, leaving his left arm exposed at the wrist. Struggling made it worse for Tyr, and slight pulses made his body shift uncontrollably. He was now standing upright, his body wrapped entirely by the serpent, while the ravens swirled overhead.

The jolts from the serpent brought memories to the surface of his mind. Birds surrounding Revna during the encounter with the wolf; Revna always pressing to study in Tyr's room while randomly tossing items aside as he read the history books. The way she studied the branches against his arm, asking questions about them, questions he could not answer. She knew what a Fylgja was. The only other time he had heard the term was in his encounter with Gorm. She hadn't learned it from the history books.

Tyr felt the anger rising within him as the thoughts flew quickly through his mind. "Revna, it was you all this time. Erik had nothing to do with it."

She smiled, reaching to touch the side of his face. "It didn't have to end this way."

Tyr spat at her and felt the shock instantly; his body screamed as he tensed.

Revna walked away from him. "Get the relic."

"Gladly." The man sheathed his sword, runes illuminated on his arm, and a seven-foot troll appeared, with tight gray skin, long, lanky arms, and tusks jutting from below its nose.

The troll reached forward and grabbed the relic, pulling.

Stars danced in Tyr's eyes, and black dots appeared at the edges of his vision. Excruciating pain rushed through his body. The serpent pulsed and sent his nerves into overload. *"Revna!"* he cried.

Her back was turned to him as the troll continued to pry the relic from his hands.

"*Helena!*" he cried within his mind. "*Help me!*"

"*Fornyel—*" The warmth and words died before completion as the air shattered about them. The troll dispersed into the chill wind, which knocked the man back into the rocks, where he went still.

A wooden spider shifted in the air, slammed against the snow, and dashed toward Tyr.

A raven's claws grabbed the square wooden spider, and the spider's tendrils lashed at the raven's body, sending it as dust into the wind. The spider landed gracefully, regenerating its tendril legs, and jumped toward Tyr's hand.

The serpent recoiled, blocking his hand and bringing its thunderous gaze before him. Lightning echoed about the rocks. The spider went limp, and its wooden tendrils dissolved as the square relic went still in the snow.

Tyr felt the serpent relinquish its hold on him. An axe appeared at the back of its neck as it dissolved into the air. He fell to his hands and knees, agonizing pain pulsing about his body.

He heard Erik yell from behind him, "Revna!" He staggered in front of Tyr between the relic and Revna. "You're going to—go through me!"

Tyr gazed up to see Erik facing down Revna in the Kriger defensive stance.

"I'll leave," she said.

Tyr tried to yell for Erik to watch out, but his words slurred together.

The fox rushed through the snow and slammed into Erik's knees, sending him to the ground. Revna was there as he caught himself on his shield, her knee colliding with his jaw.

Erik rolled to the side, eyes rolling into the back of his head.

Revna rubbed her hands against the leather leggings, picked up the relic, and knelt beside Tyr.

"It didn't have to end this way," she whispered.

He tried to grab her, but he was too weak to do anything. She kept pushing his hands away.

"Gorm can't have the relic, and since we've both been exiled, come find me in Mork Skog." She bent down and kissed him on the cheek. "For what it's worth, I'm glad that we were close. Goodbye…for now."

Tyr tried to follow her, but his limbs couldn't carry him forward. "Revna…" he whispered. She moved away. His bloody hand was covered in puncture wounds where the relic had been, and they oozed with every inch he moved. Then he collapsed beside Erik, the light dimming around him.

# Chapter 15: The Aftermath

"Fornyelse. Vakne Tyr." The voice was melodious. As it spoke, he felt the warmth throughout his body, particularly in his left shoulder. "Fornyelse. Tyr, vakne!" The voice rose to a crescendo "Fornyelse!" He could feel his body gaining its strength back.

The grove was empty before him. The tree had started to wither and die, and the pond was devoid of life. Mist filled the gaps between the decaying foliage.

His steps crunched against the broken branches and dead leaves as he stepped toward the benches, which had collapsed and crumbled away.

"Helena!" he called. "Helena." His steps were quick as he darted to and fro about the grove. It was empty now. The life had drained from it.

"Child," came a soft voice.

Turning, he found a shadowed version of Helena, the green hair now replaced with withering brown strands. Her lush green eyes were dimming to dark brown. Her bark skin peeled and crumbled as she moved toward him.

He rushed to her side, catching her as she fell. "Helena, what's happening?"

"Oh, child." She reached to touch his face. "You've grown stronger than you know. Without the relic, and the further away it goes, the more it takes from me." She coughed, and leaves fell from her hair.

"I can't go on without you. There is so much I don't know about who I am." Tears streamed down his face. "Please, don't go."

"Fortify yourself, or all is lost." She glided her hand across his face, the vines withered before him, and she collapsed in his arms. Her body crumbled into dust, caught in a gust of wind.

"Helena!" he yelled, and he could see the darkness creeping toward the grove. "Helena, I need you! Helena, I call you and bind your will to mine."

The ground shook, and the earth swallowed the stones about him.

"You dare try and bind me!" Helena stood before him, her shadowed frame in the dust cloud. The dust burned before him, displaying her body. "Weak, pathetic child!" Her dusted hand, covered in flames, struck his face.

The light reached down, lifting his eyes open. Tyr gazed at the clouds overhead. Elevating himself off the ground was the first step in getting out of the mess he was in. The snow had stalled, awaiting the storm that was heading in. Light filtered through the clouds overhead, each broken apart, allowing small light beams to break through.

Tyr's face stung where Helena had struck him earlier. Specks of skin upon his face felt the burning sensation. He found Erik on his back in the snow and inspected him for wounds he could cover. The bolt that had struck him had gone sideways through his leather breastplate, and he had a thin gash across his underarm and chest. Besides that, he seemed unharmed.

The man who had summoned the troll and nearly gutted Tyr was gone. Revna too.

Erik stirred rapidly off the ground. "Where is she!" he shouted.

"Gone. Let me help you up." Tyr reached a hand to help him. "She took the relic with her."

"No…no, we need to get back and tell Njal." Erik started moving about anxiously.

"I'm not going back to Njal," Tyr said. "I'm going after Revna."

Erik stopped moving and turned to face Tyr. Then he grabbed Tyr by his breastplate. "You can't abandon us."

Tyr knocked his hands away. "Without the relic Gorm isn't going to let them go. It isn't my problem."

"Your problem?! You would leave Liv to die at the hands of those monsters?!"

"I'm one of those monsters. Didn't you see what Njal

did to us?!" Tyr yelled. "He was going to slaughter us like the rest."

"How can you say that?" Erik lowered his voice.

"He never gave me the chance to explain my side of the story. My being a Vokter was enough to make him bring his axe down." Tyr picked up his axe and shield. "I would ask you to do me a favor."

"I owe you nothing," Erik spat. "I saved your life and put mine on the line for you, and you turned your back on your people, even your own mor. Take your favor to the trolls."

Tyr knew he deserved that. Erik had stepped in front of Revna to protect him at the last moment, when she could have gutted him. The practice duels they had done growing up showed that Revna was superior with the shield. A true shield-maiden.

The rationale of leaving the connection to his past in Revna's hands was unbearable. She was walking away from the only piece that could give him the answers he dearly sought. Leaving Liv wasn't an easy decision to make. But he knew he would only be in the way of the others. Njal had set the tone of how they treated anyone who was a Vokter. None of the Krigere had spoken to him while they held him prisoner.

Erik was different. On the other hand, he had been able to set aside the knowledge of Tyr's being a Vokter and save their lives, knowing it would tip the scales in their favor to have two on their side of the battle.

Revna's betrayal had deepened his open wound of trust. Regardless of how Erik pleaded for his help now, Tyr had made his decision.

"Take care of Liv after you bring them home. For me." Tyr asked his favor regardless of how Erik felt.

"Do it yourself!" Erik stomped his foot. "I have my own family to save. I can't believe that I don't even know you anymore. Years of devotion to family, and you turn your back on her. At least tell me why."

"She isn't my true mor. She is out there somewhere, I can feel it."

"Your mor abandoned you."

Tyr moved quickly, shield slamming toward Erik. Their shields connected. "There has to be a reason she did, you half-troll."

Calls came from over the rocks, calls for Erik. Tyr lifted his finger to his lips. "Don't say a word."

Erik held his breath, lips closed tightly, then parted them slowly. "You've made your choice then?"

Tyr nodded.

"Glem det!" Erik muttered angrily. "Have it your way." Then he called out to the others.

Tyr slammed his shield against Erik again and turned, running in the opposite direction from Erik.

Then he saw his fur sticking up out of the snow. He rushed toward it and found his totems. Yanking them out of the snow, he discovered his wolf-pelt shoulder pad and lucky rabbit's foot. He held them tight, rushing away from Erik.

Then he saw Gertrude spot him from around the rocks. Erik pointed at Tyr, and they ran toward him.

He was never going to outrun them. Exhaustion caught up to him as he trudged through the snow with each step, the gap closing between them.

Being betrayed once again by Erik made him angry. He used that anger to keep moving forward, holding the totems tightly against his chest.

The realization almost made him miss a step. His Fylgja. He called to Catori, holding the fur tight against him. The runes flared to life, and the enormous wolf appeared beside him, fur shifting in the wind. "*We need to get away from this place, now!*" he screamed in his mind as he ran alongside the wolf.

"*Get on!*" The growling voice rose in his mind, and the wolf stopped, lowering herself to the ground.

Tyr turned, seeing Gertrude with wide eyes, her rush increasing. He held his belongings tightly in his left arm against his shield. His other hand grabbed the tuft of fur behind Catori's neck and hauled himself atop the wolf.

Catori sprinted away, each step expanding the gap between him and the Krigere chasing him, though he heard them curse his name as he left their sight.

"*Head southeast toward Mork Skog. I seek vengeance,*" he told Catori.

# Chapter 16: The Path Divided

The calm morning wind rushed through Tyr's brown hair as they rode through the snow back toward Kjarra and Mork Skog. The wolf heaved and pushed quickly through the snow, covering a reasonable distance before slowing.

"*We need to keep going. Don't slow down,*" he told Catori.

Catori stopped and lowered herself to the ground. "*I need rest,*" she responded, and she faded beneath Tyr and vanished into the air.

Tyr fell two feet into the snow where Catori had been, and he hurried, glancing over his shoulder to where he thought he would see the Krigere chasing him.

There was nothing but clear snowy hills, the mountains looming to the west, and no sign of life around.

Tyr dropped the totems to the ground, then began strapping them to his body. He wondered why Catori hadn't continued.

Helena had mentioned the reserves of the totems before their use. Once again, she had left it up to interpretation for how to do those things.

He draped the blue wolf paw over his shoulder with

the claws dipping down, strapped the rabbit's foot to his waist, and held his shield along with the sheathed axe in his hand. He was ready to continue moving southward.

He thought about the reserve that Helena had talked about. He reached toward the wolf paw with his mind and felt nothing. Empty.

The rabbit's foot brought Kanin to his heart. He could feel the presence close and dear to him when he thought of Kanin and reached mentally toward the rabbit's foot. It felt very close.

"How can I test this?" he asked himself, looking for a way to understand what Helena had been trying to teach him.

Thinking of Helena, the beauty of her features, the green vined dress, and her flowing green hair made him feel her presence. His eyes went wide. She was still there, somewhere, but it felt like such a great distance. Her last words told him that the relic was going farther away, which had caused her to fade.

Distance. He thought about the feelings within him. Catori felt nowhere. Kanin was very close, while Helena was very far but there.

Harnessing Kanin, he dashed yards ahead quickly. Then he relinquished the hold on his totem. Reaching toward Kanin, he felt the distance grow between them.

Kanin was there, but the distance wasn't upon his heart any longer. It wasn't close as it had been previously.

Harnessing it again, he then checked the distance growing between Kanin and himself.

The psychic feedback he had accrued was from harnessing the totem before checking the distance between Kanin and himself. Though this time he hadn't received the feedback when harnessing it.

It was time. It had been a while since Tyr had called to Kanin, and it was intense.

Helena had been telling him all along. The way she had to rest, the leaves gliding to the ground as she spoke the words dear to his heart. Fornyelse. Simple words that had given him the strength he could have never found on his own.

Reaching for Helena, he could feel the distance between them, and it was tugging at him from the southwest. Mork Skog. He continued on his path to find Revna.

Being alone had started to break down mental walls within him. Would Njal be able to save them without Tyr's help? He knew the strength of the Krigere and had won the first war with the Voktere nearly two decades ago.

There was nothing Tyr could do to help Njal and the others now. Without the relic Gorm was going to kill them all before they ever reached Eski. That was why Njal and Odger had wanted the relic off Tyr. They knew it was hopeless otherwise.

He knew what his path was now: to finally learn about his past. The stinging worry nagged his thoughts as he tried to place walls between his ambition and his mor.

Was he going leave Liv to die by Gorm?

His worry started to consume him. Was he truly going to give up on his mor and chase something that was never there? Stopping in the snow, he pulled his hair. The anger was present with nothing to unleash it. He gazed back to Eski. He should go and help. Fighting within himself built the rage, and he screamed.

The rage slowed from the anger leaving his voice, and he found himself staring at his feet. He bowed his head forward into his hands, trying to calm himself.

They didn't care about him. He'd been betrayed by his friends, was haunted by his past, and had lost the respect of his elders. The acceptance was gone.

He moved his hands to scream into the sky, then saw something dangling from his neck.

The Eter-Tree. "Treasure life," she had told him. Treasure the moments spent in this life instead of those things not worth chasing. He lifted the Eter-Tree necklace as it unfolded before him. Liv. His mor had given him the life he couldn't have asked of anyone. He had honestly forgotten it all—the Warrior's Gate, the prophecies, and most of all, his mor.

He dropped the necklace, turned toward Eski, and harnessed Kanin, kicking the snow up behind him.

They had been there all along, leading him to what he held closest in life. Then he started to recite the prophecies he had received at the Warrior's Gate.

"Courage, strengthened through adversity—intuition to embrace the unknown. Tough decisions lie before you—conviction in the veins. Honor shall guide your thoughts to determine right from wrong. Spoken words lead to action."

It had strengthened him throughout the last couple of days, learning more about pieces of his past that had been unknown to him. All of the decisions he had made believing they were right and following his instinct, yet he had started to make the wrong one by following Revna instead of saving those he loved most.

He felt ashamed that he hadn't allowed his thoughts to flow freely, giving them space to determine right and wrong, but the last words hit the most as he recited them. "Spoken words?" The names he had given his Fylgjur. Their names were power.

"Ambitious. Decisive. Competitive. No fear of the

responsibility placed upon your shoulders. However, I see your heart shall become divided. You will become restless, and I know that you will sacrifice those you love most to achieve a long-lost dream."

The division in his heart was evident in what he had gone through. He had been willing to sacrifice those he loved most to learn about his past.

He continued to resolve the guilt he felt as he recited the words of the prophecy, as his hold on Kanin vanished. His steps slowed, and he pressed forward, continuing with the last prophecy.

"Faith. Consistency. The pattern of the past shall shape the way of the future. Inner manifestations tell you of what you are becoming. Without fortifications of character, then all will be lost. Patience empowers your understanding."

Helena. She had told him what he was becoming, and he could still hear her utter the word *calm* inside his mind. He had lost his patience for trying to understand and giving time for things to happen on their timetable.

He should have listened to her, not pressed against the leskes she had been teaching him and prodded her for answers. She had told him to be patient and wait for the right time.

The burden started to fall from his shoulders as he

continued to look for deeper meaning from the words of the prophecy. He found what he needed now to press toward Eski.

Backtracking the route he had just taken to leave the Krigere behind, he made his way back toward the rocks. His reserves of Catori had started to come back closer to his heart, and Kanin had been returning too. Helena felt further away, and it felt that his grasp was slipping in having any hold on her now.

He saw the rocks he had escaped from and headed north, away from them. He looked for any sighting of the Krigere or any watchmen who would catch him off guard.

His belly ached from the lack of food, and constantly pressing the snow into his mouth for water had become tedious. It would be hard to catch any wildlife for food with his axe and shield, but his eyes continued to search for any game about.

He caught a glimpse of brown fur near a small grove of trees. He eased his way toward it, hoping to find an animal left behind, but as he got closer, he saw a woman lying on her back in the snow. His heart sank. The gray hair blended into the snow, and frost had begun to form on her face.

"Liv!" Tyr screamed. He harnessed Kanin to close the distance and rushed to her side.

He dropped his shield and touched her face. It was ice cold, and he lifted her hand into his. "No…Liv, Mor!" he screamed, tears streaming down his face.

Her hand moved in his, gripping him. Then she coughed. "Tyr?" she asked.

"Yes, it's me." Tyr smiled at her, tears in his eyes as she looked up at him. "What are you doing out here alone?"

She coughed, lips blue. "They separated me from the others…" She coughed again. "Then chased me out into the cold with their beasts and told me to find my son."

"I'm here now, and we need to get you warm." Tyr reached under her. She threw her arm around him, and her face was close to his.

She gazed into his eyes. "Are you and that girl together yet? She would make a great wife, you know…" Her strength left her. She coughed and fell back into his arms. "I want to see you happy." She squeezed his hand. "Treasure life with her. I love you, my son."

"I love you too, and don't say such things." He started to lift her off the ground, and she went limp in his hands. "Mor?" he called, shaking her. "Mor, no!"

She was gone.

# Chapter 17: Eski

Night had fallen upon the city of Eski. Clouds rolled in from the northeast, blocking the moon and starlight. Torches burned within the city walls, braziers were topped with wood that burned for hours, and snow crystallized into flakes and fell with the great winds of the storm.

The Voktere were posted at the west, east, and south entrances into Eski. The ocean's waves north of the city slushed their way forward, with ice forming atop the calm waters. The waves crashed against the docks in the harbor, pushing against the shores of Eski.

The city's walls extended into the waters, protecting the city from invaders, and only had three main entrances. The west and east had smaller openings in the walls meant for getting in and out of the city quickly. Still, anyone invading the area would have to squeeze through the entrances one person at a time, which allowed the guards along the wall to pour hot boiling tar on invaders, rain arrows down upon them, and spear them as they entered the city.

The braziers burned away the snow and reflected off the snow upon the ground. The shadows of movement within the city gave away the positions of the Voktere.

Tyr knew it was on purpose, and he welcomed the

challenge of facing them all in combat upon the open ground.

He had moved Liv, covering her with her brown fur, and left her near the grove of trees, hidden from sight. The tears had streamed down his face as he relived tender moments with his mor. She had provided him the best life she could, never complaining. Liv had always looked happy. He had covered her with fur, giving thanks for all she had done. Then he'd moved to prepare for the battle before him. No matter the pain, sadness, or misery he felt. He was going to make them pay, and he had already started to control the rage burning within as he waited for the night to come, when he could avenge those who had suffered at Gorm's hands.

The plan Njal had conferred with the Krigere about had commenced. Voktere fell on the walls to wicked bolts slung through the snowy currents, which brought them low to the ground.

They moved on the east and west entrances. No alarms sounded.

Tyr found a place to lie low outside the walls, out of sight, waiting for the plan to be executed. He saw the Krigere moving forward, only shadows from this distance, and then they moved beyond his sight at the walls.

Three Voktere were stationed at the main entrance in

a triangle formation, one in the front, one left, and one right.

Tyr was alone, with bottled rage, axe, and shield at the ready. He wasn't going to be sneaking into the city. He wanted them to know where he was.

He was going to live the Kriger virtue: no fear of death.

Tyr walked forward. Wind and snow dashed past him as he entered the torchlight. Once the Voktere spotted him, they shouted, and one lifted a horn to his lips. Then the horns within the walls sounded, and the Voktere turned back to the city, then back to Tyr.

Harnessing Kanin, he burst into motion. The blurring of snow and hard footfalls brought him to the first Vokter. He slashed his axe across the top of his knee, and the Vokter bent forward in pain. Then Tyr slammed his shield across the side of his face and hopped to the right past him.

The other Vokter ran toward Tyr. Runes flared upon his armor, a wolf on the right and a bear on the left.

Tyr threw his axe using the speed of Kanin and then relinquished his hold on Kanin as it left his hands. His steps slowed, and he called to Catori and willed her toward the Vokter on the left.

He buried his axe in the Vokter's chest. The wolf vanished in the wind.

Catori ripped right through the Vokter. Her claws raked through his armor, and she bit into his side. Then the bear vanished to the wind.

Catori vanished when Tyr dismissed her. "*Well done,*" he praised her, and she disappeared.

Tyr walked toward the Voktere, yanking his axe free. He wasn't going to give them time to get the jump on him. He knew that he could be quickly overwhelmed if they had a chance to summon their Fylgjur.

The walls were twice his height, made of dark rock and mortar. Moss covered the once bountiful city, which had been abandoned nearly two decades prior. He stepped past the large wooden gates that lay splintered in the snow from the last war.

Largely abandoned homes were near the city entrance, and the commotion of war rang from farther in. He could hear the shouts and screams of the battle raging.

He continued toward the homes and shoved their doors open. He found the first empty and continued to the next. He could see the Fylgjur and Krigere engaged in combat. The mastery of the Krigere with their axes and shields dashed the Fylgjur before them, dispersing them into the snowy wind.

Njal led the charge from the west, while Odger brought the Krigere with him from the east. Wounded were brought into the center of their shield formation as they pushed toward the center of the city.

A shadow passed against the hut, and Tyr turned, his shield brought up. The sword bounced off it. Tyr swung his axe, and the Vokter jumped back, Tyr's axe hitting air.

The smell hit his nose, and two large gray hands barreled toward him. He brought his shield tight against his arm. The blow knocked him back into the hut. Pain erupted as he slammed into the stone wall.

He fell to his knee with a quick breath, eyes upon the troll and Vokter moving toward him. He called to Catori, giving her his instructions, and harnessed Kanin.

The blue wolf appeared before him, leaping toward the troll.

Tyr ran straight behind Catori as she took the troll aside, his shield before him. The Vokter moved to avoid the wolf and found Tyr sprinting at him.

Tyr brought his shield hard against the sword and brought his axe down.

The Vokter fell, and the troll vanished with his last breath.

Dismissing Catori and relinquishing Kanin was Tyr's first step after moving past the fallen Vokter.

Tyr checked the distances with his totems and found

that they had started to grow farther away. He couldn't keep doing what he was doing. Eventually he was going to get caught alone.

His eyes found the well surrounded by a grove of trees, and then he spotted the large tree alone off to the side, and the recited words from his childhood came to mind.

"It is so with us, the Krigere. We become better individuals, more useful timber, when we grow together rather than alone. Let us grow together."

The battle raged on beyond the well. Tyr couldn't see Njal and the Krigere with him past the grove of trees, but he heard their war cries. More of Odger's Krigere fell to the onslaught of the Voktere and their Fylgjur.

Tyr bit down on his lip and cursed to himself, then rushed toward Odger and his kin.

Tyr found the backsides of the Voktere nearest to him and cut them down where they stood, their Fylgjur vanishing. Odger had shifted his shield wall toward Tyr, then found he had started to assist them and readjusted further.

"Where is Njal!" Tyr yelled after moving into the shield wall formation.

"Should be coming through those trees any moment!" Odger yelled back. "Hold formation and press!"

The Krigere held their positions as the Fylgjur circled and pounded against the shields. Trolls, wolves, and bears sat outside the shield barrier, their numbers dwindling as the Krigere opened their shields enough for an axe to slide through and then retract.

Tyr felt the fists of a troll hit his shield, and the Krigere next to him fell to the bolts flying in. Tyr stepped in to fill the gap.

He saw the Krigere behind him, two wounded and one dead from the crossbow bolt that had struck his shield.

"We need to get to the Voktere and end this!" he yelled over the fighting.

"What do you have in mind?!" Odger asked.

"You aren't going to like it!" Tyr said. A smile rose to his face. The realization hit Odger a moment later, then he nodded.

"On Tyr's command!" Odger yelled to the Krigere around them holding their shields in formation.

Tyr pressed his shield against the formation, then willed Catori out. The large blue wolf appeared behind him, and he yelled, "Charge!"

The shield wall parted in the center, and Catori rushed through. The troll was knocked back, and the way was paved. The Krigere rushed forward in the wake of the blue frenzy and took down the Voktere, along with their scattered Fylgjur.

They converged on the well and waited for Njal to emerge on the other side.

"Demon spawn," Odger told Tyr. "Thought you had come to wreak your revenge on us when I saw your mad berserk rush toward us."

"Forgive and forget. My mor taught me that," Tyr told him, grabbing his necklace. It wasn't going to be easy to forget what they had done to him, but Liv would have wanted him to.

"Doesn't change what you are," Odger shot back.

"Did you find any of the hostages?" Tyr asked, trying to prevent the conversation from going any further.

"Nah, just those demon spawn." He spat back toward the dead Voktere.

"Njal said he would be meeting you here?" Tyr asked.

"Yes, but the silence is giving me the willies."

"Help!" A child's voice broke the air through the trees.

The Krigere moved in proper formation through the trees. Tyr could see the braziers burning bright in the distance as they progressed through the grove. The trees, along with the heavy snow, made it hard to see past anything without stepping through each tree.

Voices could be heard ahead as they exited the grove.

"Let them go, Gorm!" Njal yelled. "I'll give you my

life for theirs."

Njal was unarmed and being pulled by his arms by two giant trolls. The other Krigere were missing. He was alone. Tyr saw Elsie standing beside Gorm, her hair wrapped in his hands. Tears streamed down her face.

"Ah, just the man I've been looking for." Gorm saw Tyr step out from behind the trees. "Come to see your chieftain die?"

Tyr couldn't see Njal's face, but Njal lowered his head in defeat as the trolls held him.

"I'm the one you wanted. Here I am." Tyr moved forward and shoved past Odger. When Odger tried to stop him, he whispered, "On my cue."

Seeing the way Gorm held Elsie by the hair boiled the bottle of rage within Tyr. Nothing was going to stop Tyr from preventing Gorm from hurting his kin, and if he could give his life to save theirs, then so be it. "You tried to kill me once and failed. I'd like to see you try that again."

The Voktere shifted, moving to a better formation as he moved toward them. Tyr could see five of them.

He looked for the other hostages. If Elsie was here, where were the others? Then he saw what he needed.

"She is just a little girl. Let her go. It's over. It's me you wanted," Tyr said, lifting his shield and axe away from his body. He was to the side of Njal where he could see his face now.

"Stop where you are and drop your totems!" Gorm screamed, his open hand before him, and the trolls pulled on Njal. He screamed in pain.

Tyr dropped his shield, then unbuckled his fur-covered leather armlet and dropped it to the snow. Tyr questioned if Gorm knew what were possibly totems and what weren't. He lifted the rabbit's foot from his belt, dropped it to the snow, raised his hands, and flashed the Kriger salute. "Done."

Gorm's eyes went wide, and he closed his hand into a fist, pulled the girl's hair, and rushed away.

Odger had taken the cue and moved forward while all eyes were on Tyr. He had seen Erik and Gertrude waiting in the shadows, and now they emerged, taking down one of the Voktere controlling one of the trolls.

Njal screamed as the trolls pulled at his arms, and then one vanished. The other troll took the force and fell backward, its hands wrapped on Njal's arm.

"Njal!" Tyr grabbed his axe and tossed it over to Njal. Njal grabbed it out of the air and sent the troll into the mists.

The rest of the Krigere and Voktere were in heavy combat with each other. Tyr strapped the rabbit's foot to his waist and started toward Gorm, but Njal stopped him and handed Tyr back his axe.

"This isn't over between us," Njal said. His large frame seemed weary from the ordeal, and his graying black hair was crusted to the side of his head with blood. He was missing one of his metal shoulder pads. Only the one on his right shoulder was left.

"I know," Tyr said and continued after Gorm, leaving the rest of the Krigere to face the Voktere. Njal joined them in the fight.

Tyr reached the docks and witnessed the scene before them. Gorm stood on the central dock leading out toward the slushing, snow-covered waters as the waves crashed along the wooden structure and shore of Eski, his hand wrapped around Elsie's hair.

"It's over." Tyr stepped onto the dock, the wood creaking beneath his weight. "Let her go."

"It was already too late to execute the hostages when I found out that Revna had taken the relic for herself," Gorm said, pulling the girl's hair. Cries erupted from her petite frame, and tears ran down her face. "Selfish girl."

"Help me!" Elsie called.

Tyr stepped forward. There was no way around Gorm to reach her, only forward.

"Don't you see that you're one of us now? Why turn

on your kind?" Gorm asked.

"Hurting innocent people? No thanks." He continued forward.

"Stop right there." He walked toward the edge of the dock, leaning Elsie toward the slushing waves.

Tyr stopped, hands out, gesturing Gorm to stop. "There isn't anywhere to run. It's over."

"We had it all planned out, and that foolish girl!" he roared in frustration, hurting Elsie further in the process. "She ruined it and left me here to die."

Revna had told Tyr that she couldn't give Gorm the relic. She had helped Tyr in her way. But the betrayal still stung.

"What do you want?" Tyr had his hands up to show good faith.

"What do I want? What I have always wanted! Justice for being exiled from my own family," Gorm said. "Didn't my brother tell you?"

"Your brother?"

"Don't you see the family resemblance?" Gorm waved his free hand over his face.

Tyr looked at him and saw the features of the man from whom he had wanted acceptance all his life. Njal.

"Ah," Gorm said. He could tell that Tyr saw the resemblance. "After all these years, he thought I was dead, only to find out that I was still alive thanks to you.

He was born without the gift of the Voktere, and when we started to force the wills of the Fylgjur, he tried to stop us and went on his campaign to rid the world of every Vokter bloodline. Even your own."

Tyr lowered his hands. His true parents had been Voktere, and Njal had killed every last Vokter he had found.

He looked back and saw Njal and the other Krigere reaching the docks. The other hostages were safe. He could see Berner standing beside Erik and Gertrude, holding a Vokter sword. They were all safe—all except his mor, whom he had left outside the village.

Had Njal killed his mor and far to erase the Voktere from the face of the earth? Leaving Tyr an orphan to never know his actual past?

Njal looked at Tyr, and Tyr's rage boiled over.

"Did you kill my parents?!" Tyr yelled at Njal, walking away from Gorm.

"What are you talking about?" Njal called from the shore.

"My parents, they had to be Voktere since I have the gift. Did you kill them?" Tyr closed his fists, tightening his grip on his shield, then reached for his axe.

"I don't know who your parents were," Njal said.

"They didn't matter to you!" he yelled. "Revna was right; your pride and arrogance blinded you to the destruction you wreaked."

"It has." Njal lowered his head. "There is no penance equal to the pain and suffering I have caused, even to my own."

"Now that you know what I am, you have rejected me as your kin, bound me as your prisoner to accept a fate that you feel justified to perform?" Tyr asked him, determined to get an answer.

"I worried when Liv brought you into our village. After all the bloodshed of my people, bringing in a child that might possess the gift troubled me." Njal stepped toward Tyr. "It may have been wrong for me to pass judgment on you so quickly. When you grew into a man, I treated you as I would a son. You are Kriger to me, though that changes nothing of what you are now."

Tyr lowered his head so that the Eter-Tree necklace dangled freely. The past was immutable, but the future could still be written. His mor had taught him that, and he didn't doubt it. "This is far from over between us."

"Never said it was," Njal responded.

"No!" Gorm yelled. "He killed your family, and you're going to let him get away with all that he has done?"

Tyr glanced back at Gorm, hearing a splash in the water. Gorm still held onto Elsie's hair. Regardless of how Tyr felt about Njal and the Krigere, he was one of them, and Gorm needed to let the child go.

"It's over." Tyr walked toward Gorm, then heard a rushing wave strike the dock with a large object.

The serpent rushed out of the water and coiled around Tyr. His shield and axe dropped to the deck and into the water.

The gentle pulses of electricity rushed through his body while the serpent coiled around him, and its eyes faced him once more, the thunderous storms billowing in them as his life was being drained from him.

Helena was gone and wouldn't be able to bring him back to life as she had in the past. He was alone, and after Gorm had finished with Tyr, Elsie would be next. Gorm was trapped and eventually would lose to the oncoming Krigere from the shore, but Tyr couldn't let that happen.

He let his rage explode, pushing against the serpent. The shocks continued as the pressure built. Then he called to Catori.

The dock shifted under the heavy weight as the wolf sank her teeth into the serpent's scales. Catori threw the serpent toward the shore and leaped after it.

Catori thrashed at the serpent as it tried to wrap itself around her body. The furious fight scattered the Krigere and sent them backing away as the two battled on the shore for dominance.

Tyr had dropped to the dock after the serpent relinquished its hold on him and rushed toward Gorm, harnessing Kanin.

Gorm chucked Elsie into the water. She screamed as she fell, and Gorm started to pull his sword from his sheath. Tyr threw his left tree-woven arm into Gorm, knocking him back into the dark waters. His sword flew through the air, then Tyr dove into the waters after Elsie.

The waves crashed about as he searched for Elsie, toppling head over heels in the freezing water. He brought his head above the surface and saw her gasp for air, then swam toward her, barely grabbing her before the next wave crashed into them.

He held tight to her as they went under the water. As they came up, he found himself pulled away from the dock entirely. He swam forward, pulling Elsie behind him and pushing her onto the dock as another wave pulled him under.

He surfaced farther away from the dock and saw the serpent and giant wolf fighting one another. Elsie had made it safely to the dock, and the Krigere were throwing furs around her. He could hear them yelling at him, and he swam as quickly as he could but was pulled under again. The cold water had numbed him, and he felt himself growing tired.

The ice and slush rocked against his skin as Kanin

drifted away, the reserve empty. Another wave crashed over him, and he stopped struggling.

He felt the water crash beside him, a heavy pressure tight against his back, then cold air once more before he blacked out and closed his eyes.

# Chapter 18: The Return

It was four days since they'd left Eski and returned to Kjarra. Before Catori had vanished, she had gone into the water and brought Tyr back to the shore, where the Krigere then took him over to the burning braziers to get warm.

When he had awakened from his chilled sleep, they had already started to leave Eski behind. He urged them to stop and gather all of the Vokter totems before leaving, informing them that he had to release the spirits bound to them.

Through their exhaustion, the Krigere went about gathering all of the totems until Tyr was satisfied.

They had created a makeshift wagon to bring the bodies of the dead home, and they picked up Liv along the way south back to Kjarra.

Berner and Elsie rode beside Tyr, asking him questions about the big bad wolf they saw fighting the serpent. The last couple of days had left him exhausted, in and out of sleep, only to wake to more questions. Elsie wanted him to show her a troll, and no matter what Tyr told her, she insisted. Berner asked if Tyr would train him to be a Kriger when they got back, and he was very determined to beat Tyr one day.

Njal told Tyr that they hadn't seen any sign of Gorm

after he was knocked into the water. The serpent had vanished into the waters before Tyr was saved by the wolf. Njal asked that Tyr keep the knowledge of being a Vokter to himself. Keeping his spirits away, Njal said, would be the best way to help heal the wounds in the coming weeks. After their discussion, they rarely spoke to one another while the Krigere rebuilt their village day by day.

The triumphant return home brought the sounds of horns and cheers of all the Kriger people. They mourned the loss of the fallen and buried them. Then they celebrated their return and the lives of those who had passed on.

Erik's and Tyr's relationship started to mend as they discussed the events over the last couple of days. Erik wasn't the spion that Tyr thought him to be. It turned out that Revna had been the real spion, helping Gorm get into the village to take the hostages.

Erik had gone with Tyr to unbind the Fylgjur from a fair number of totems they had gathered off the Voktere back in Eski.

They knew that over time their friendship might return to what it once had been. The trust just needed time to mend.

Tyr went to Sif to get all the books on the Vokter and Kriger war. Then he dove in, trying to learn all he could about the Voktere. He had to keep himself awake to read the long, boring history on each page, but he knew it would be worth it.

Tyr knelt beside the grave dug for his mor and saw the many trinkets people had left for their loved ones against the wooden grave markers. They would spend time creating more permanent stones to mark each of the fallen.

His mor had given him everything. She had raised him to be who he was: strong, determined, and kind. He was going to miss seeing her beautiful face each night when he came home to dinner. He remembered what she had said to him at the Warrior's Gate.

"Tyr, my son. I am proud and honored to present this necklace to you. As your mor, I am blessed by you."

He bowed his head, lifted the Eter-Tree necklace, and responded to her words. "No, Mor. I was blessed to have you and honored to be your son."

On his way home, Tyr found Njal standing outside his replaced door. He carried a shield and axe along with an old book.

"Chieftain Njal." He saluted as he approached.

"Tyr, son of Liv." He bowed, his hands full. "I came

to bring you a new shield and axe since you lost yours."

Tyr accepted the gifts. "Appreciated."

"I also brought you this." He pushed dust off the corners of the book where he had missed it. "My mor was a Vokter and my far a Kriger. They ran the village in harmony with one another. Then the Voktere started an uprising when told to stay true to the Vokter ways. My parents were killed during the conflict, and it left me hopeless. I ran my brother and the others out of town, then decided to rid the world of the Voktere.

"My parents kept this book to keep the teachings of the Voktere alive. They wanted to pass the knowledge down through the generations." He handed the book to Tyr. "I could never make myself burn my mor's handwriting, but it had always been nagging at the back of my mind. After seeing who you had become, I thought it best for you to carry on the traditions left by my mor."

Tyr glanced down at the book and slowly turned the pages. Countless words were written throughout, with drawings of creatures and detailed notes. He closed the book, excitement running through him. "Thank you. This is what I have been looking for."

Njal smiled. It might have been rare to see such a hardened man smile, but it was a sight to behold. "I know. Sif said you had been asking about books on the Voktere. At first I thought it was insane that you'd be asking to read voluntarily, and we had a good laugh about it. Then I remembered the book, hidden away for nearly two decades." He lay his hand on Tyr's shoulder. "I accepted you as a Kriger and was wrong to ever doubt your loyalty. Now I entrust one of the most sacred pieces of my past to your hands. Bring harmony back to our people as my mor and far did in the past and bring justice to those who are determined to take it away."

Tyr nodded. "I will bring that harmony back to our people. It may take time to rebuild what your parents did in the past, but if we work together, we can accomplish what they wanted."

Njal tapped his shoulder. "Thank you." Then he started to walk away.

Tyr called for him. "Njal. I'm going after Revna."

"I know, and you'll always have a place here to call home. I owe Liv that much." He nodded and walked away.

Tyr rushed into his house and closed the door behind him. He lit a small candle on a makeshift desk he had made for himself, shoved all the books aside, and set down the one Njal had just given to him.

It was going to be a long night. He turned to the first page. He needed to learn before heading to Mork Skog after Revna, and he was determined to do it. Without

Helena to guide him, the book would have to do.

# Epilogue

Agnar stood at the pond conversing with his water nymph when the doors to the throne room burst open.

"Drott Agnar, I tried to stop him." The Vokter stood at the door as Gorm shoved his way into the throne room.

He could see Gorm's serpent wrapped around the Vokter's troll. He waved his hand, dismissing the water nymph. "It's all right."

The troll burst into mist, and the serpent slithered into the throne room past the Vokter before vanishing altogether.

"Welcome, Thegn Gorm." His deep voice sounded across the stones as he turned to greet him.

Gorm bent to one knee. "Drott Agnar." He bowed his head in respect.

"What news do you bring in such a fury?" Agnar asked.

"I've failed you, my drott. The young man still lives, and Revna betrayed us, abandoning the plan and taking the relic for herself." Gorm looked up at him.

Agnar paused for a moment; why would the girl do such a thing? He thought about why she would betray them. "Interesting." His voice was soft, and he reached down. "I doubt that the girl would betray us—but leave us, now that I could believe. Did she say why?"

"I think that she took a liking to the young man." Gorm got off his knees. "I plan on leaving tonight to go after Revna."

Agnar threw his hand forward. "No! That Fenrix is back and has been attacking our defenses. He needs to be dealt with, and I need time to process this riddle. Leave. I'll send for you when I am ready to proceed."

Gorm bowed. "Yes, Drott Agnar."

The door slammed behind him, and Agnar walked back to the pond within his throne room. He reached up and touched the skull upon his left shoulder, caressing it. "Don't worry, my dear, you'll soon be reunited." He flicked his right hand out, fingers rolling outward as runes flared upon his armlet, and the water nymph reappeared before him in the pond.

CPSIA information can be obtained
at www.ICGtesting.com
Printed in the USA
LVHW080913140922
728278LV00004B/719

9 781958 071007